BRAZEN ROGUE

TAMARA Gill

COPYRIGHT

BRAZEN ROGUE, The Wayward Woodvilles, Book 8 ©
2022 by Tamara Gill
Cover Art by Wicked Smart Designs
Editor Grace Bradley Editing, LLC

ISBN: 978-0-6457257-8-0 (trade paperback)

PROLOGUE

1807, Davion Hall, Derbyshire

Bellamy held his daughter in his arms, stared down at the little cherub cheeks and pouty lips, and could not help but smile. What a beauty she was.

"What shall we name her?" he asked Sally, his wife of only a year.

Sally sighed, leaning into the many cushions at her back, and closed her eyes. "I do not care what you call her. I'll leave that decision for you," she said, disinterest and annoyance in her tone.

Bellamy shook his head, wondering why she was so dismissive of him, and now their child, especially after her determination to gain his hand in marriage. To gain the title of marchioness seemed paramount to her only last Season. So much so that he and others were hurt by her actions. Not that she seemed to care, which appeared to be a trait of hers he'd come to dislike.

"What is wrong with you?" he asked her, moving over to a chair and sitting. "I have tried so many times to make our marriage work, and even now, when you have given birth to our child, you are cold and unfeeling."

"I never longed for children. You knew that," she spat, her lip curling up when she glanced at the babe. What little feeling Bellamy had for his wife vanished at her blatant dislike of the child.

"It's an occupational hazard when a wife seeks their husband's bed. You knew a child was bound to occur."

"I had hoped I was barren."

"Another point you should have disclosed before you tricked me into marrying you. There are plenty of gentlemen who do not want children, but I require one to continue the line of my family. I disclosed such before we were married, and you were in agreement. How changeable you are now that you are the Marchioness of Lupton-Gage."

"Little that has given me," she snarled. "We're always stuck out here in the Lake District. We never entertain, and it's dreadfully boring. I do not see my friends or hold balls and parties. You're practically keeping me hostage."

Bellamy stared at Sally and wondered if she had finally lost her senses. "You are free to go to

London whenever you wish. I have never stated otherwise."

"Well, perhaps I might. I need a little distraction, and now that the child is born, I'm free to do as I please."

"Within reason," he cautioned her. "I do not want to claim a child that is not my own. Remember that, my dear, when you entertain in Town."

She shrugged, her face mocking. "You would never know. For all you know, the child you hold is not of your blood."

A cold chill swept down his spine, and he narrowed his eyes on his wife, wondering if she had been unfaithful to him. He glanced down at the small bundle of innocence in his arms. She had the Lupton-Gage dip in her chin as all of them were renowned for having, not to mention her coloring was identical to his as a child, or so family portraits claimed. No, the child was his. Despite how much his wife wished that were not the case. "No, she is mine, and if you do not wish to be here, I will not stop you from leaving. But it still eludes me why you fought so hard to become the next Marchioness of Lupton-Gage since the title revolts you so much."

She sighed and rolled to her side, giving him her back. "You know why. I had to marry a man of wealth and status, or my family would be ruined. You fit that bill better than most and were the easiest to deceive."

Bellamy stood and left the room, taking the child with him. He would not listen to another minute of her venomous ramblings. He remembered that night all too well. Having received what he thought was a missive from Miss Reign Hall, he had all but run to the music room at the Collins ball, only to find Lady Sally Perry there instead.

She had thrown herself at him, tried to kiss him, and while in the throes of removing her, her brother had stumbled upon them, all by design.

Disgraceful behavior and the end of what he had wanted most.

Reign Hall ...

"Prepare the marchioness's luggage. She is leaving and traveling to London as soon as she's recovered. Please hire a wet nurse post haste and move the child's nursery to the room across from mine. I wish to keep her close should I be needed."

"Yes, my lord," his butler said, sending several maids to do his bidding.

Bellamy waited in the room he would make his daughter's, walking the small little babe to the window to look out over her home. "All will be well, little lady. I will give you enough love that you will not miss your mama. I promise you that." He kissed her soft forehead, thankful to have her at least.

If he had to endure a loveless marriage, at least he had a child. That was better than nothing, and he would cherish and love her always.

ONE

1812, Grafton

Reign hugged her closest friend the Marchioness of Chilsten in her modest parlor, happy that she was in Grafton visiting her parents and willing to come to spend some time with her.

"What is this I hear about you going to live and work in the Lake District? This cannot be true. You must come back to London with me, and I shall sponsor you for a second Season," Julia pleaded, taking her hands and squeezing them as if that would change her future or her mind.

Reign shook her head. Her friend, happily married since '07, glowed from wealth and privilege, while her circumstances became direr with every year.

Her parents had passed over the last two winters, and now she was responsible for their small cottage and farm. While she had many skills, keeping a working farm was not one of them, and she had sold off what land she owned to keep from starving.

"Julia, I know you care about me, and I care for you. But I can no longer stay in Grafton. The work that I procured here is not sufficient. There are not enough families in need of a governess, and or cannot afford to pay one's fee. I must go. The position in the north will be good for me. I shall have room and board. I'll be fed, and the little girl I'm to look after is of a sunny disposition from all accounts."

"But the Lake District is so far away. I will never see you," Julia said. "Please reconsider. I'm certain that we can find a good match for you if you come to London."

"No, my friend," she said, Julia's large diamond earbobs catching her eye for a moment. Merely one of those diamonds would keep her fed, clothed, and the bailiff from her door for a year or five. "I'm determined to make my own way in life. I have a plan. This cottage will soon be sold, and I'm going to save as I've never saved before in my life before booking passage to the Americas. They write that there are opportunities for men and women if one is willing to work hard. And I'm willing to do so. I shall not shirk my duty, and perhaps I can be successful over there when I cannot be here. That is what I hope in any case."

"America?" Julia gasped. "You'll be killed, robbed, or mistreated, and I shall not be there to help you. You cannot go, Reign. I forbid it," Julia said, fear lurking in her almond-shaped eyes.

"No, I will not be. Do not be so dramatic. I will earn enough money here in England before I book any passage across the Atlantic, enough to keep me well for many months before I find employment."

"I do not like this idea of yours at all." Julia paused, biting her lip. "And what of this place you're to be a governess? What is the family like? Do I know them?" she asked. "Do I like them is possibly a more important question to ask."

Reign chuckled. How she loved her friend, and if she could wish for things to be different, she would, but she would not be a burden to anyone. Life had dealt her some troublesome cards, but she wasn't shy about working on getting herself out of the little pit of pity she lived in.

"A married couple named Davion, I believe. The office in London that referred the position to me said if I were willing to travel north, I would be tutoring a little girl of almost five years who required guidance and learning."

"Why does the name Davion spark a memory in me?" Julia said, frowning. "I will keep thinking on the matter and shall let you know if

I remember. I think when going into a position as you are, the more you know of the family, the better."

Reign picked up the small bell on the table and rang it. Her cook, who also acted as her housemaid, knew the notification for tea and biscuits.

"We shall have tea and discuss the matter some more. But for now, tell me of everything that you have been up to. I must know all."

Julia smiled as she started to speak of her family, her children, and everything that had happened since she had seen her last. Reign reveled in her friend and all the happiness that marriage to the Marquess of Chilsten had bestowed upon her.

Once she had wanted the same, and there was a time during her first Season when she thought she may have won a gentleman's heart. But it wasn't to be, and now she had to make her own way in the world. No matter how lofty her connections were, that did not make her any more wealthy, and she would not depend on charity. As long as she drew breath in her lungs, she would make a life for herself through her own toil.

And that journey started in the Lake District.

REIGN STARED UP AT THE LARGE, imposing estate that the carriage driver from Rowsley had delivered her to.

This was Mr. and Mrs. Davion's home? The house had to have one hundred rooms, if not more, not to mention the grounds, extensive and manicured to an inch of their life. It was not what she had been expecting.

She knocked on the door, her small valise in hand, and waited for a footman to answer. A house of this magnitude had servants, possibly hundreds of them.

And now she would be one of them too. She hoped they would accept her and be friendly. Even though a governess or lady's companion was seen as a more elevated position in the household, she did not want that for herself.

This far north in England, she did not know anyone, and she already missed Julia. A friend or kind word was what she desired above anything else, and she could only hope she soon had a friend or two.

"Yes?" a droll voice asked as the door swung wide to reveal an elderly man with jowls hanging on either side of his cheeks.

"Hello, sir. I'm Miss Reign Hall. I'm here for the governess position for the child of Mr. and Mrs. Davion."

The elderly retainer raised his brows before his mouth closed into a displeased line. "Side door leads into the kitchen. All staff enters through there. I shall meet you in the kitchen shortly and announce you to all the staff."

With those words, the door slammed shut in her face, and Reign swallowed the lump that formed in her throat. Never had she been met with such rudeness, nor had she ever seen any of her friends speak to their staff as this man had spoken to her.

Was this how other servants treated one another below the stairs?

As instructed, she moved off the front door steps and started for the side of the house, choosing the left, as it seemed a more sensible side to the house for a kitchen to be situated, not that she knew the workings behind her thoughts.

Thankfully her musings were correct, and she soon found the kitchen door open wide and several staff coming and going from a garden a little farther down the path.

"Good afternoon," Reign said to two maids in the gardens, thankfully both returning her greeting. A better start than she had at the front door. She knocked on the open kitchen door to find the angry man who had met her just before with a busty woman with a deep scowl, a long, black dress, and a pristine white apron standing at his side. The housekeeper, perhaps?

"Miss Hall, welcome to Davion Hall. I'm

Mrs. Watkins, and this is the butler, Mr. Watkins, my husband, whom you met just before."

Reign sighed in relief that Mrs. Watkins did not seem as prickly as her husband. "It is a pleasure to meet you both," she said. "I look forward to meeting the child I'm to care for."

"Yes, Lady Alice is a lovely child, but in need of tutoring. Come in, and I shall show you about the kitchen and then your room upstairs. As you'll be looking after Lady Alice, there is a room beside the nursery that you may use for the duration of your stay."

"Thank you." Reign said before she was introduced to multiple people, the cook, several footmen and maids, the chambermaids, and one of the grooms, who sat at the table having lunch.

"These are the servant stairs, they travel up to the attics, and you may use these instead of the main staircase unless you're escorting Lady Alice."

"Of course," Reign said, following the housekeeper, whose tour of the house was quick but efficient. "This door leads to the front foyer of the house," she said as they climbed up to the ground floor.

The housekeeper opened the door for Reign, and she stepped into the foyer, looking up at the grand staircase made from marble. Several doors led off into multiple rooms that she would soon become accustomed to, she supposed, the longer she was employed here.

"This level houses the dining room, library, back and front parlor, music room, and conservatory. You may use any of the rooms, bar the dining room and library."

Reign nodded, taking in all that she could with the hasty tour.

Now that she was here, she realized she knew very little about the family and what they desired of her. She hoped she made a good impression and was able to stay, move forward with her plan and earn a good, sound wage.

America and its possibilities beckoned her, and she did not want anything to scuttle her dreams, not even if it meant she had to work as a servant for a year or two to accomplish them.

Two

Bellamy stared down at the parchment in his hand and quickly wrote out a response to his steward to send funds to yet another of his wife's traveling locales she departed without paying her debt.

Since her death two years past, letters such as the one he received were often, and he paid them, not wanting any menacing whispers that the Lupton-Gage family did not deliver what they owed.

Even if that debt were not his but that of his late wife, he would deal with the matter and move forward. His wife was renowned for causing strife wherever she went and leaving unpaid accounts seemed to be a hobby of hers upon arriving on the continent. He would not allow anything to shadow his daughter's future in society, not even one IOU.

His housekeeper Mrs. Watkins' loud and commanding voice sounded in the foyer along with that of a young woman's. He glanced at the date and realized the new governess for his daughter was to arrive today, and that is with whom his servant must be speaking. He leaned back in his chair, debating whether he felt up to greeting the young woman from the South of England or not.

He supposed he ought since she had traveled a great distance and he was not an ass most of the time. Not to say he did not have his moments ...

Their voices dimmed, and he knew they had headed up the stairs to the first floor. His daughter would be in her room, waiting for him to collect her for their daily ride. She would be finished with her lunch by now.

Bellamy stood, striding for the door, and started up the stairs. He caught sight of the housekeeper and the young woman she was escorting heading toward the picture gallery, and he strode to his room, needing to change into his riding attire.

His valet came out of his closet, used to the occupations and times he kept, his riding gear already in hand.

"I thought the brown breeches and tweed jacket best for today, my lord," Chambers said.

"Very good." Bellamy stripped off his jacket and took the tweed from his servant. "Do you know if Alice is dressed for our ride?" he asked.

"I believe I saw a maid enter with her lunch and remain to help her change as usual. She will be looking forward to today, my lord. Are you not teaching her to jump a small log in the north field?" Chambers asked him.

Bellamy frowned and turned to his valet. "How do you know such details?" he asked. "I have told no one of my plans."

"Ah," Chambers said, tapping his nose. "Lady Alice has been telling everyone since your ride yesterday that you promised her this. Please do not go back on your word now, my lord. She will be most displeased, and we shall all have to hear about it."

Bellamy laughed, knowing that for the truth it was. Alice, his darling little girl for all her beauty and wit, was a termagant. "I promise I shall not disappoint her and therefore subject you all to her displeasure. She will be content and happy after her ride, so long as she keeps her seat."

"Ah yes, well, let us hope that she does," Chambers said, folding the breeches he removed. "Have a pleasant ride, my lord."

Bellamy strode into the passage with a nod and ran directly into a warm, lithe woman's body. He reached out without thought, clasping the woman's hips to stop her from tumbling to the floor.

With the force of their joining, her face slammed into his chest, stealing his breath.

"Apologies," she mumbled against his shirt, disentangling herself from him and stepping away. "I did not see you there, my lord."

"Oh, my lordship! I do apologize," Mrs. Watkins lamented over and over. "We did not expect you to ... to ..."

Bellamy waved the housekeeper's words aside. "It does not signify. I did not see you either and should have taken more care." He smiled at the young woman, having a good look at her finally, and felt the blood drain from his face.

It could not be ...

The pit of his stomach clenched, and he felt his mouth gape. He closed it with a snap, forcing his heart to stop racing. That the young woman's face, too, had paled and was possibly the mirror image of his made him feel a little less conspicuous, but not by much.

He knew her.

"Reign?" he croaked, clearing his throat, so he did not sound like a total imbecile. "I mean, Miss Hall? Is that you?" he asked again, unable to tear his eyes from the woman he had once hoped to call his wife.

She was as beautiful as he remembered her. Long, brown locks, the darkest-blue eyes he had ever seen. Eyes that had once looked up at him with such hope, the affection he had sought, but now ...

Now they looked upon him with horror.

His attention dipped to her gown, a little dusty from travel, and aged. Where had she been for the past five years? It shamed him that he had not inquired with the Marchioness of Chilsten during the few times he was in Town.

But he could not allow gossip to sully his name. His wife had enabled that enough, and he did not want his daughter to be harmed any more than she already was by their association with a woman who had never wanted a husband or to be a mother.

"Lord Lupton-Gage?" She glanced at his housekeeper as if she would confirm such honorifics. "I was told this house was for Mr. and Mrs. Davion." She shook her head, clearly confused. "I apologize. I do not understand how such an error has occurred."

Bellamy wanted to take her hand, comfort her, but he restrained. "Davion is my family name, Bellamy Davion, Marquess of Lupton-Gage. When I inquired about a governess for my daughter, the hiring office in London must have misread my missive when they replied to you," he said, wondering how such an error could have occurred. He was certain he had addressed his correspondence correctly.

"Oh," she said, her eyes weary. "Apologies,

Mrs. Watkins. His lordship and I know each other from London. We met many years ago during my Season in Town."

"Really?" the housekeeper said, her eyes flaring wide. "I did not know governesses had Seasons in London. I thought you said you were from a small village named Grafton."

"I am, that is true," Miss Hall said, frowning. Bellamy could see she was upset, concerned by this turn of events and what it would mean for her downstairs. "Before my parents' passing, they had saved enough money to give me one Season, but unfortunately, I did not receive an offer of marriage."

Her eyes briefly met his, and shame washed through Bellamy. Although he had not asked Miss Hall for her hand, he knew from their time in London that she cared for him. Their one stolen kiss that, to this day, haunted his dreams. He had liked her very much and knew without a whisper of doubt that emotion would have grown into love had it been given the opportunity.

"I'm sorry for your loss," he said, listening to his housekeeper say the same. "As for Miss Hall and my past being interconnected, please do not notify the staff of such things, Mrs. Watkins. If Miss Hall is to be treated equally, I do not want anyone to think there is differential treatment merely because we're acquainted. Am I understood?" he asked, knowing his housekeeper had an uncanny ability to gossip.

"Of course, my lord. I shall not say a word," Mrs. Watkins stated adamantly.

"I do apologize, my lord. Had I known I was to work at your estate, I would never have accepted the offer," Miss Hall said, working her hands before her.

"All will be well," he said, waving her concerns aside. "We did not know each other well in London," he lied, ignoring Miss Hall's fleeting glance. "But I'm glad you're the governess of my daughter. Being the good friend of the Marchioness of Chilsten, I know you will give Lady Alice a well-rounded and proper teaching."

She nodded eagerly. "I will, my lord. I shall not let you down."

He gestured toward his daughter's door. "Let me introduce you to Lady Alice. I'm about to take her riding in any case."

REIGN TOOK A DEEP, CALMING BREATH and hoped that she did not appear as startled and shaken as she felt. Her heart thumped loudly in her ears, and heat kissed every part of her skin. She clutched her hands together to try to stop their shaking.

Mr. Davion was Lord Lupton-Gage? Bellamy?

How could such a mistake occur, and how was it that of all houses she was to work at in England, it would be the one of the very man she had once harbored feelings for?

She closed her eyes briefly, following his lordship and the housekeeper into the little girl's room.

Once harbored feelings for? Who was she kidding? After five years of being apart, knowing he was married, and still her heart beat too fast whenever she thought of him. And now being under the same roof ...

How would she ever remain disengaged when the man she had loved and lost was near her every moment of every day? Just as she had dreamed for far too long.

Entering the room, she took the opportunity to study him. His hair was a little longer, and there was more stubble across his chiseled jawline, but his dark-blue eyes were the same. Still held that look that only she recognized; a lost opportunity and regret for what had been stolen from them.

She could not stay here. To stay would mean temptation. She was a woman well on the shelf, a wallflower, and now a governess with no prospects, no family, or funds to speak of. She did not need to be around temptation when that temptation was married. No longer hers to admire and long for. To whisk into darkened gardens and kiss under a moonlit night.

She had lost him years ago. She could not take him back now, no matter how much she may wish to.

They entered a room that was front facing of the estate, with a large bank of windows, two open to allow the warm breeze to float inside. Reign smiled at the nanny, who sat on a rocking chair, reading a book, as a little girl dressed in riding attire sat on a wooden horse, rocking keenly and listening.

Upon seeing him, she squealed and ran over to his lordship, where she was hoisted up and spun about.

Lord Lupton-Gage kissed his daughter's cheek and smiled at her. Reign had never seen such a handsome smile in her life. For all the weeks she had known him in London, she had never seen him so happy. It was clear as the sky outside on this sunny day that the marquess loved his daughter dearly.

"Lady Alice, let me introduce you to your new governess, Miss Reign Hall. She is a lady whom I once knew, many years ago in London, who's to be your friend and guide and teach you. I hope you will be extra gracious and listen to everything Miss Hall has to tell you," he said, meeting Reign's gaze a moment, his attention dipping to her lips.

She swallowed the nerves that fluttered in her stomach at his look. She had seen that hunger before and recognized it well. That look had given her the courage to kiss him one balmy night in Town, and what a kiss it had been too.

"Hello, Miss Hall. Thank you for coming to teach me," the little girl's sweet voice said. She glanced back to her father with a small grin on her lips as if to seek his approval.

Which, of course, she received. His lordship was gracious to his little girl, it seemed. "Very good, Alice," he said.

Reign dipped into a curtsy. "It is lovely to meet you too, Lady Alice. I look forward to getting to know you and having our lessons. I'm certain we shall have lots of frivolities together."

"Not all levity, I hope," the housekeeper interjected. "Lady Alice must be intelligent and learned. We cannot have all fun and games afoot," the older woman said, her voice brooking no argument.

"Of course, Mrs. Watkins." Reign dared not say anything else. She would have to ensure they had such activity when not in front of the housekeeper.

THREE

Bellamy excused himself and Alice and started for the stables. His heart beat far too fast for his liking, and he needed to go outside to get away from the temptation that was Reign Hall.

He may be a widower now, a man still young and virile, but he was not looking for a wife. He had suffered under the late Marchioness of Lupton-Gage and was not seeking to renew the role.

But Reign was nothing like Sally.

Where his wife had been cold and calculating, Reign had been warm and direct, not to mention loving, amusing, and sweet.

Hell, he had adored her.

He adored her still.

He ran a hand through his hair and inwardly swore. What the bloody, goddamn hell was she doing as a governess?

How the hell had such a blunder occurred?

"I hope it does not rain today, Papa," Alice said.

He turned and smiled at his daughter, whom he was still carrying. Deciding she could walk, he put her down, and she ran along at his side. "I'm certain it will rain at some point, but we shall make the most of it until it does," he said.

They arrived at the stables to find Misty, Alice's little pony, saddled. She lunged, more than ready for her afternoon ride.

As usual, Alice refused help into the saddle, preferring the mounting block instead. Bellamy let her go, willing to let her have the freedom to decide what was best for her. Without it, she could not learn.

He led the pony to the north field and unhooked the leading rope, allowing her to walk about the small, fenced area. For several minutes she walked and trotted before taking the pony up to a fallen tree log for the horse to study and sniff.

"She's very clever for a five-year-old," a feminine voice said at his side, startling him.

He turned to find Miss Hall staring at his daughter, a small smile playing about her kissable lips.

He took a deep breath and forced his attention back to his daughter. His body rioted, burned that she was beside him again, near him as she always should have been.

How had he not sought her out after his

wife's death? How had he forgotten the sensations she brought to life in him whenever he was around her? Whenever he thought of her.

"She has been riding since she was three. Of course, her nanny did not approve, nor did the household, if I'm being honest. All were worried she would topple from the saddle and hurt herself, but she did not. I do not allow much, but I will allow her to try to jump the small log, and as you can see, it is barely ankle height."

Miss Hall chuckled, and he drank in the sound. It had been so long since he'd heard her laugh.

He could still recall their first dance, and he instantly became besotted with her. He bit back a grin. Actually, that was not quite true. The day he had seen her huddling in the bushes at Hyde Park, and his carriage had splashed her gown, well, that was when he knew she was the one. Her annoyance and anger at him ruining her gown for days after had been telling.

She had spunk and did not care that he was a marquess far above her rank. He liked that about her.

"Be careful, Alice. Hold tight the reins, along with the mane, and do not forget to tighten your knees when you go over," he called out to his daughter.

"Yes, Papa," she called back, turning her pony

away from the log so she could have a proper run-up.

"I do not think I could allow my child to do what you're doing. I hardly know her, and I'm nervous," Miss Hall admitted, a concerned frown between her perfect brows.

He inwardly sighed, drinking her in, wishing for things that could never be. "All will be well, Miss Hall," he said, hoping what he declared was true. His daughter turned her pony around and pushed her into a slow canter before jumping the log easily and without nary an issue.

"I did it, Papa," she called.

"Oh, thank God for that," Miss Hall said, her hand across her chest.

Bellamy chuckled, clapping. "Well done. You're a natural, my girl."

They watched for several more minutes as the pony was made to jump over and over again the small log. The little horse never bothered by the monotonous action.

"I'm sorry about all this, my lord," Miss Hall said at last, her voice low. "Had I known this was your home and sanctuary, I would never have come here. Not in a million years."

Bellamy shook his head, not wanting her to feel ill at ease. "I'm sorry too, but there is nothing to be done about it. You're here now, a governess, and we shall make the best of the situation. I'm certain you will do well tutoring my daughter."

He stared down at her, wondering what had become of her. To his shame, even during his marriage, he had dreamed of her. Had woken hot and unsatisfied, longing ripping through him like a knife.

"You left London so suddenly I never got a chance to explain ..." He paused. "What have you been doing these past five years?"

She stared out into the riding yard, and he saw she followed his daughter's progress. "I returned to Grafton, my parents passed away, and I found out my father was not as frugal as he ought to have been with the finances. There was not enough money for me to have a second Season, even though Julia did offer to sponsor me, but I could not allow that. Too much pride, you see," she said, laughing at her own words.

He did not laugh. He found what she said held little amusement. If anything, it read like a story of sorrow and anguish, not to mention fear. "And so you became a governess?" he asked.

"Yes, for two local families in Grafton, but they were not so much better off than I was, and my conscience would not allow me to take a wage when I knew they scrimped and saved to pay me each week. But I also could not work for nothing. I wrote to an employment agency in London, and they informed me of this position in the Lake District, and here I am," she said, shrugging.

"And here you are," he repeated, wondering

how he would keep from watching her as he once had in London. To his shame, he had been a little obsessed with her then. Until he was tricked into marrying Lady Sally Perry and his affection for the woman at his side was forced to end overnight.

"I'm sorry for your loss and your hardship. Although I do hope your income of £30 annually is adequate," he asked her.

"It is more than generous, thank you," she said, her cheeks turning a soft shade of pink.

"I'm glad you are here, and I can help you in this small way. We were friends once. I hope we may be so again," he said, having never meant anything more in his life. Their situations so changed now meant that friendship was all that was open to them both, but he would take it. He hoped she would too.

She met his eyes, and he marveled at the color of hers. Like a deep, stormy ocean, so many secrets and hidden treasures. "You are my employer, my lord. The time for us to meet as equals has ended. I hope you will not mind that I think it best to keep it such a way."

He nodded, understanding all too well what she was saying. Their time had come and gone, and this was certainly not a second chance. "Say no more, Miss Hall. I agree wholeheartedly, and no harm done."

. . .

Reign breathed a sigh of relief just as Alice started to walk her pony toward them. "When would you like me to start the lessons, my lord? I can commence today if you wish," she asked him.

"No, tomorrow is fine. It will be dark soon, and you still have to unpack from your journey, and I'm certain you will be tired. It is a long way from Grafton to Derbyshire."

"I suppose you are right, and I think I shall sleep soundly this evening," she said. Already her legs ached, and her eyes were itchy. The idea of a bed, of lying on a soft mattress and not a jarring carriage over rough roads, tempted her, and it was not yet dark.

"My daughter dines with me every night, so feel free to eat in your room if you wish, or belowstairs with the servants."

Reign nodded, knowing she would have to get used to being belowstairs instead of an upstairs guest as she once was. How fickle life was that one could feel as though the stars were hers to capture and now to wonder how she would pay the butcher for the beef.

"I shall go belowstairs. I do not know anyone, and as you know, for several years now, Julia has lived in London. I have missed the company of others to gossip and talk to."

"It is amusing that you mention such things. Up here in the Lake District, we have many neighbors, but we rarely get together. You have arrived just in time, for in a fortnight, I'm to hold a house party for the first time in several years, and there will be an influx of people and staff. You will have more than your share of people to speak to."

Reign smiled, wondering if he had forgotten so soon that she would not speak to any of them as was her position in life now. "And will Lady Lupton-Gage be in attendance? I have not yet seen her," she asked, wondering where the marchioness could be.

His lordship's face hardened, his eyes narrowing in thought. "Lady Lupton-Gage left after our first year of marriage, and I received word while she was abroad that she passed in a carriage accident."

For a moment, Reign was rendered mute. Lady Lupton-Gage had died? Why had Julia not told her such news? But then, did she even know? From what she could gather, his lordship had not traveled from Derbyshire for some years. Mayhap no one knew.

"I'm so sorry, my lord. I did not learn of the tragedy," she said, placing a little space between them, not wanting a servant to see them together and suspect her of trying to win his lordship's affection, knowing he was a widower.

How mortifying such a rumor would be, and she needed so desperately to fit in here, to earn her keep and survive. She could not have disgrace touch her.

"Thank you," he said, striding to his daughter, who joined them, a wide smile on her pretty face. "You did so well, my darling. You are a grand horsewoman," he said.

Little Lady Alice giggled, and Reign smiled. "Thank you, Papa. I think I have earned my cream cakes at dinner this evening, do you not think?" she stated.

"I think you may well have," he agreed, smiling over at Reign. The pit of her stomach clenched seeing him again, outdoors, happy and grinning. He was so handsome, so lovely, and had been hers once.

Why could he not be again?

No, she inwardly swore. Widower or not, he was not for her. But oh dear, if only he were, how sweet her life would be.

Four

The next day Bellamy sat in his library and listened to the sound of the pianoforte and the soft melody of Beethoven drift through the house.

Miss Hall was playing, instructing his daughter, who now and then tried to replicate Miss Hall's delicate touch on the ivory keys, but to no avail.

Somehow Bellamy knew that music was not his daughter's forte.

He picked up the missives that had arrived today, several acceptances for his house party and one in particular that he knew Miss Hall would be pleased to know of.

Not that he would tell her. As his daughter's governess she would not expect to be informed, but having the Marquess and Marchioness of Chilsten arrive would please her and put a welcome smile on her pretty face.

A letter stamped from Spain caught his attention, and he tore it open. The last known location of his wife was in Spain before her passing, and although he had been advised of her death, he did not like that he had not been able to bury her here in England and allow his daughter to say goodbye to her mother, to visit the grave whenever she wished.

There was something fundamentally wrong with such a thing.

The missive explained yet again another debt that required his attention. An inn where she had ordered an unhealthy amount of wine if the inventory of her bill was any indication.

His daughter's chuckle and that of Miss Hall's reached him, and curiosity got the better of him. He stood, moving toward the music room door that was just a little farther along to his library.

He leaned against the threshold and watched his daughter try to read the music and play at the same time, Miss Hall guiding her, never chastising her or correcting her when she made an error. Which, unfortunately, was often.

"I'm only five, Miss Hall. I'm certain with your teachings, by the time I'm five and a half, I'll be proficient."

Bellamy bit back a laugh and noted that Miss Hall, too, was fighting not to chuckle. His poor daughter missed her mama, even though she had never known her. And he knew she longed for the company of women or one woman who would love and care for her.

It was the one thing he could not forgive Sally for. Even with her lying in the cold hard ground as she was.

"Lord Lupton-Gage, I did not see you there," Miss Hall said, standing. "Come and listen to Lady Alice. She is doing very well."

He smiled and joined them at the pianoforte. His daughter sat up straight and corrected her fingers before starting to play. "Do you see, Papa? I'm already getting better. Miss Hall is a wonderful governess."

Miss Hall smiled but did not reply, and nor did Bellamy. It was odd being near her again. Awkward and yet also not. He wanted to speak to her, have long conversations about all things, and yet he could not. She was a governess now, a different social sphere to his, and there was no changing that fact.

And they had not been alone in some years. So many things had changed in both of their lives.

But that long-ago kiss ...

His attention moved from his daughter, and he met Miss Hall's eyes over her head. She had taken control that night, had clasped him by the lapels of his coat, and stolen the kiss she wanted.

What they had both wanted.

The moment their lips met a firestorm of need—pent-up desire—had ripped through him, and there had been no turning back. He had denied his feelings and what she had come to mean to him, but after that kiss, there was no denying what he felt.

That Lady Sally Perry had taken note too, and had put a stop to their courtship soon after pained him to this day. Miss Hall had returned to Grafton, and that was the end of that.

"You played beautifully, Alice," he said when his daughter finished her song. "Tell me, what else have you planned for the day?"

His daughter all but bounded on the piano stool, her eyes alight with excitement. "We're going to have a picnic, Papa. Down near the river and Miss Hall is going to help me catch frogs. Real frogs that will jump and everything."

For a moment, Bellamy had no words for such a thing. He looked to Miss Hall and found her watching him curiously. "Real frogs, Miss Hall? Are they not more appropriate for boys?"

"Not at all, my lord. Lady Alice requires learning of all things, not just painting and embroidery," she said. "Nothing that I had not done when I was her age," she added, smiling down at his daughter, who beamed back.

"Miss Hall," his daughter chided. "I thought we agreed I'd be Alice from today onward."

"Of course, sorry, Alice," she said, grinning at his daughter.

A warmth settled about his heart at Miss Hall's words. A little girl who longed for the attention of a mother and had never been given such a treat. A day out to picnic and rummage for frogs would be a dream come true for a five-year-old.

As much as he had tried to be both parents to Alice, there was nothing quite like a mother's love, and he wished she could have had everything she deserved.

"Did you want to join us, Papa?" Alice asked him, reaching up to clasp his hands and shake them a little. "You can help too. If we catch one, then I may get a treat?"

"A healthy treat, my lord. An apple from your orchid that's warmed in the sun, not anything bad for her," Miss Hall was quick to interject.

He smiled. He had no engagements this afternoon that would stop him. "I would enjoy coming down to the river with you, Alice. I shall go and change and meet you down there if you like?"

"Yes, thank you, Papa," she said, jumping from the stool and running toward the door. "I'll have nanny change my clothes directly, Miss Hall," she said before her governess could utter a word of reply.

He shrugged, meeting Miss Hall's eyes. "Had your lesson ended? I fear my daughter seems to think it so."

Miss Hall chuckled as she packed up the music and the pianoforte, a sound that made him wish for more of the same. "We had been playing for some time, and Lady Alice is only five. Her attention span is not so great yet, so it is best, I find, not to push her too much." She paused, glancing toward the door before meeting his eyes. "Are you certain you wish to join us? There may be mud involved this afternoon, my lord," she warned him.

He waved her concerns aside, walking her to the door. "Do not worry about such things. I think you forget that I was a boy once and more than capable of catching myself a frog or two."

"Very good, my lord. I'm glad that I shall only have to teach one of you then," she said before leaving him alone in the room.

He watched her leave, shaking the melancholy that assailed him each time they separated. He strolled back to his library. Their time had come and passed, if they ever had such a time, and now it was time to move forward.

He had Alice to think of. Marrying his governess and raising yet another scandal in his life was not something he could do.

No matter how much he may want to.

* * *

REIGN TOOK OFF HER BOOTS AND stockings and left them on the grassy bank beside a tree where she hoped no little green jumping frogs would look for refuge from their exploring.

They had looked through the grasses and some rocks, and yet still, they had not found a frog. They could, however, hear their little croaks, which drove Alice to distraction, running about trying to find where the sound originated.

The sound of a twig breaking made her look up. Her mouth dried at the sight of Lord Lupton-Gage sitting on the grass, stripping off his socks and shoes, exposing the lower length of his legs and his feet.

She had never seen a man's feet before and there was something oddly masculine about it, so very different from her own.

"You will not find any frogs there," his lordship declared, striding down the hill to join them. "But these rocks I have always found particularly promising." He led them over several large boulders to a group of rocks semi-immersed in mud and a little flowing water.

"Come, Alice," he said, helping her to move one rock. "I'm certain there will be frogs under here."

Reign joined them, leaning down to peer under the rock as his lordship rolled it to the side. The squeal of delight that Alice let out rendered Reign deaf for several moments before a little frog, moving in the mud and water, came into sight.

"There is one," Alice gasped, reaching in to pick the little frog up.

Reign bit her lip, peering at the little frog who was completely adorable. "How sweet they are, and so tiny. We should investigate what kind of frog this may be and research it, Alice," she suggested.

"I would say it's a Rana temporaria," his lordship said, peering at the little amphibian. "A common frog in England. I do have a book, as a matter of fact. In my library, Miss Hall. You're more than welcome to borrow it," he offered.

"Thank you, that will be most helpful."

"Shall we look elsewhere?" he suggested to them both. "Maybe we can find more. How would you like that, Alice?"

Lady Alice nodded eagerly, placing the frog back where it was when they found it, but before his lordship could lower the rock back to its original place, it jumped up and landed in Reign's bodice.

She screamed, reeled backward, and landed with a thump in the mud. Forgetting the ruination of one of her best gowns, she rummaged in her bodice, trying to fetch the little critter out.

Alice laughed and stated she would keep looking, unaffected by Reign's predicament. Reign let out another squeal as the little frog moved, sliding against her skin like a wet, slimy glob of who knew what.

"Let me look, Miss Hall," his lordship said, kneeling beside her.

Reign gasped and pushed his hand away. "You cannot! What if someone sees, my lord?" she said, her hand now down a good portion of her gown.

"There is no one to see," he said, moving closer to ensure privacy.

Reign met his eyes and could see he was in earnest. She sighed and glanced over her shoulder. Seeing no one about them, she dropped her hands at her sides and allowed him to do what he suggested. His finger pulled at her bodice, and he peered into her gown. Heat kissed her cheeks, and desire tore through her.

She wanted his hands on her. She wanted so much more than his hands, for that matter.

"I can see it," he said, his voice gravelly and deep. He cleared his throat and met her gaze. They were so close, their breaths mingled, and she realized they were both breathing heavily.

Warmth settled in her belly, and she bit her lip, fighting the urge to take what she wanted yet again and kiss him.

The frog jumped out, landed on his lordship's shoulder, and then jumped again somewhere in the muddy mess Reign sat in.

"He is out," he stated, not moving. His attention dipped to her lips, and she felt herself sway toward him before the squeal from Lady Alice on finding another frog brought them both to their senses.

"Come," he said, standing quickly. "This way." He strode to another part of the river where to Alice's glee, they found what looked like hundreds of frogs of all shapes and sizes. Reign stood and tried to push as much mud from her dress as she could, but it was no use. It was ruined.

She washed her hands in the river and let his lordship find frogs with his daughter as she prepared the picnic basket for lunch. After an hour or so, they joined her on the lawn. Reign opened the basket, full to the brim with cold meats, bread, honey, and biscuits, along with fruits and wine for the adults and lemonade for Lady Alice.

She poured Alice a lemonade before the little girl wandered off just in front of them, searching for more frogs while eating cheese and a biscuit.

"She is lovely, my lord. How proud you must be of her." Reign could not help but think that should she have had a child, she would have wanted one similar to Alice. Such a sweet, caring, honest, and happy child.

Reign passed him a glass of champagne and stilled when he reached across the picnic basket, his thumb caressing her chin several times. Her heart jumped at his touch, and she swallowed her moan. How would she survive being near him, wanting him, but denying herself when he did such things to her?

"Pardon me, Miss Hall. You had a little grime on your cheek. Not surprising after what happened," he said, laughter in his eyes.

She chuckled, knowing how true that statement was. Even so, the feel of him, his hand upon her chin, sent a longing through her that would not be repressed.

No matter how much she knew, she would have to deny herself every day she was here.

FIVE

L ate that evening, Reign left her room when the house quieted, and Mrs. Watkins would surely be asleep. The housekeeper had told her the library was off-limits, but today Lord Lupton-Gage had said she could use the room, so she was determined to do just that.

On her way down the corridor, she checked on Lady Alice, who bathed and ate dinner after their afternoon outing and promptly fell asleep while listening to her nanny read.

Upon returning to the estate, she had heard his lordship mention that he was going out for the evening, so Reign took the opportunity to slip down to the library to find the book on amphibians that he mentioned earlier. She could not disturb him if he were not here.

Candles burned in the sconces, giving her ample light to find what she was looking for. She worked her way about the bookshelves, seeing all kinds of literature, from gothic novels to household maintenance and recipes to architecture, horticulture, and medicine.

Near the latter, she found several books on amphibians and frogs in particular.

She flipped through the pages, searching for similar frogs they had found that afternoon that she could show Alice tomorrow.

"Miss Hall?" a deep baritone voiced from the doorway.

She started at the interruption, dropping the book before picking it up hastily. "Your lordship, I apologize for being in here. I was looking for the book on frogs that you mentioned. I hope you do not mind," she said, holding the book before her as if it would ward off the emotions that always bombarded her when he was near.

It did not work. Nothing worked when it came to Bellamy ...

He waved her concerns aside, laying several letters on his desk before removing his greatcoat and throwing it over a nearby chair.

"Not at all. By all means, search and use whatever books you think will assist your lessons with my daughter." He slumped into the chair behind his desk, rubbing a hand over his face.

Reign noted the dark shadows under his eyes, and he looked to have aged several years since their picnic luncheon this afternoon. "I think I have found the book I need. I shall leave you to your business," she said, starting for the door.

"Wait, stay. You do not need to go so soon. Come, sit with me a moment. I could use the company," he said, his eyes imploring her in a way she could not refuse. Had never been able to refuse if she were honest with herself.

"Very well, if you like." Reign came and sat across the desk from him, unable not to drink him in. After years of not seeing him, being so close to the man she once thought would be her husband was a delight she had never thought to experience again. "You look weary, my lord," she blurted before she could wrench the words back. She covered her mouth with her hand, unsure what possessed her to be so familiar with him. She had no right to be anymore. She was a servant in his house and ought to know her place.

He scoffed but nodded in agreement. She thought he would scold her, but perhaps he too was finding it hard to remember her place in society had altered. "You are right. I'm terribly beat and will be abed soon enough."

Reign fought not to imagine what he would look like abed. She was seven and twenty, no longer the young, naive girl who did not think like the woman she now was. Now she longed to know what men hid beneath their superfine coats, perfectly pressed shirts, and starched cravats.

One man in particular above all others. She longed to know what Lord Lupton-Gage looked like beneath all his finery. Even now, his buckskin breeches and bottle-green jacket sprayed with mud, and who knew whatever else, looked regal and so damn alluring it made her heart hurt.

"Well, I hope you have a pleasant and restful sleep," she said, wondering when she had started to reply with inane comments like the one she just did.

He watched her, and she fought not to fiddle with the book in her hand.

"I watched you today with my daughter and could not fathom how some women are motherly, have been born as if that is all the duty they wish for in life, and then there are others." He paused, his mouth twisting into a displeased line. "Women who marry for status and titles and birth a child merely because that is what they believe is required of them and then do not wish the burden of such joy."

Reign swallowed, unsure if she ought to have an opinion on what his lordship was saying, for he was most certainly speaking of his late wife. And while she may be angry with her ladyship for ripping Lord Lupton-Gage from her all those years ago, it did not mean it was her place to disregard her memory or speak ill of the dead.

"She never wanted Alice, and my daughter this afternoon was so happy and cheerful that someone was interested in the same things she was. Even if you feigned your interest, I thank you for being kind to her. She longs for the company of a mother figure, which is something I cannot give her, no matter all my wealth."

His words humbled and alarmed her. "My affection for Lady Alice is not feigned, my lord. I think she's endearing, and I'm happy to be her governess. As a woman who has also lost her mother, I can understand the hole she may feel in her life, but I hope I can fill it if merely a little bit," she said, having never meant anything more in her life.

BELLAMY DID NOT KNOW WHY HE WAS telling Miss Hall all the particulars of his life that haunted him, but for years he had held the burden of his wife, her scandalous pursuits over the continent that would always get back to him. Letters from acquaintances who relished the knowledge they were bestowing of news on his unfaithful wife and her antics.

"Thank you for your service to my daughter and your kindness. I will not forget." He paused, meeting her eyes. "What are your plans once you complete your governess duties here? Will you return to Grafton?" he asked, unsure why the thought of her leaving made his stomach twist. He did not want her to leave. Now that he had

Miss Hall—Reign—back within his sight, the thought of her leaving him was unthinkable.

She's your daughter's governess, Bellamy. She has fallen too low for you to marry her now ...

In time he would need to marry again and beget an heir, but seeing Reign again brought home all he had lost in not marrying her when he had the ability.

Her eyes flared, and her fingers tightened on the book in her lap. "I intend to save and pur-chase passage to America, my lord. I have in-structed the local magistrate in Grafton to sell my property, and that alone will get me across the Atlantic, but I shall need money to help me sur-vive for the few weeks until I'm settled."

A cold shiver ran down his spine, and he shifted on his chair. America? "America?" he blurted, shaking his head, uncertain he heard her correctly. "But surely the money from the sale of your house will be more than ample to get you there and keep you fed and housed in the inter-im." Bellamy frowned, wondering why he would say such a thing, especially when the idea of her leaving England and never returning made his blood run cold.

What are you thinking, man? She is your daughter's governess. Yes, once, she may have been suitable, but no longer. Marrying a woman who was a servant would bring only more scandal to the house of Lupton-Gage.

And his wife had filled that quota well enough when she was alive.

"Unfortunately not," she said, her cheeks turning a pretty shade of pink. "My parents were not fond of economy, my lord, and there are debts in Grafton that will need to be paid, along with several in London that resulted from my Season. If I'm fortunate, I may have fifty pounds once everything is settled."

For the longest moment, Bellamy stared at Miss Hall, unable to fathom that a person would only have fifty pounds to their name and nothing else in the world. No family, no siblings, no home.

She had nothing, and shame washed over him that he had been part of the process that placed her in the position she now lived.

But America? What would she do should she be assaulted or robbed by a footpad or highwayman? What if she were injured or, worse, killed?

With nothing else and no one to turn to in a foreign land, she would do what all women did to survive.

Whatever was necessary.

"I'm very sorry," he said. "Let me take care of your debts, so you may travel to America sooner than planned." It was the least he could do, even though he did not want her to leave.

She threw him a curious look, and he could see the question behind her inquisitive blue eyes.

"But, if I'm to depart earlier, my lord, that will leave you without a governess, and that would not be fair to Lady Alice."

He leaned forward on his desk, drinking in the vision of her. She was so pretty, her hair down for the evening, lying over her slender shoulders. A shawl sat over her arms; she was a vision, one he wished could be his. "May I speak frankly, Miss Hall?" he asked her.

She nodded and bit her lip, sending a frisson of heat to lick along his spine. The reaction reminded him what he was about to say, although hard, was for the best. For them both.

"Miss Hall, while I think it is marvelous that you're teaching my daughter, there is a history between us. One, I believe you feel as I do, even now, and I fear it could morph into a situation that is not acceptable in our dissimilar social structures."

Miss Hall's eyes flew wide, but she did not deny his words. She sat unmoving. The only telltale sign she understood his meaning was her labored breaths that made her breasts rise and fall against her gown. He glanced down at his desk, fighting to keep himself from going to her. To wrap her up in his arms and kiss her sweet, delectable lips one more time. To tell her to hell with what society would think and make her his anyway.

"My wife passed two years ago somewhere in

Spain, and I have the right to remarry, but there are rules that must be obliged. For my daughter's sake more than my own." He met her eyes and hated himself for what he was about to say. "Had I returned to London, and you had been there enjoying another Season, there is no denying that I would have pursued you, and I would have won you, I'm certain of it. But that is not what has occurred. You have taken on a position of employment in my home as a governess.

"Our social spheres are even more conspicuous than they were several years ago, and I cannot allow any more scandal to assault the Lupton-Gage name. My daughter deserves to have a Season when the time comes and have no shadow following her slippered feet. I hope you understand what I'm trying to say. Why I think it is best that when you're financially able, you will take the opportunity to start a new life elsewhere."

She stood, and her chair scooted backward at the force. She clung to her book as if it were a shield, and perhaps it was in a way. Bellamy stood, wishing things could be different, but they were not. They had been dealt a bad hand, and now they had to play it.

"I did not come here to taunt you with my presence or give myself hope that you would look upon me with favor and ask for my hand. If you believe that is the case, I shall leave first thing in the morning. I did not even know this was your estate," she argued.

"No, I do not believe that," he said, lifting his hand to still the panic he could hear rising in her tone. "I'm saying out loud to you here now, because I respect you too much not to, that I find you as attractive as the day we met, and having you under my roof is an allure that I will not be able to deny myself forever. That you are saving, that I can help you gain your plans quicker and be free of me, is best for you. I can no longer offer you marriage, Miss Hall. The circumstances of your life make it so, but I also do not want to seduce you or ruin what reputation you have left merely to slake my lust. I'm sorry to be so blunt, but there is no other way to say what I must."

She gaped at him, and her eyes burned with temper. "You forget, my lord. There is another element to your inability to keep your hands to yourself, and that is me. I no sooner wish to be ruined than you wish to ruin me, and I shall never allow it. But I will, as you so kindly offered, accept your gift to pay off my debts in Grafton and London so I shall be able to leave. Sooner rather than later, as you say. I think is best," she said, turning about and striding from the room.

Bellamy ran a hand through his hair and inwardly swore. Well, he had certainly bollocked that all up. Now she hated him, and he never wanted that. God damn fool that he was.

Six

The next day Reign threw herself into teaching Lady Alice and made a plan as to what she would teach in the following weeks to come. Which, if her calculations were correct, was all the time she required to have enough money to travel to America.

If Lord Lupton-Gage did as he promised and paid off her debts, she would be free of this place and all the longing that rose every time she was around the marquess.

As much as his lordship's words had rattled and vexed her in equal measure last evening, he was correct. There was a simmering under the surface, a burning, unheeded longing that fired between them whenever they were together.

And as much as she would like to deny it, given the opportunity, she would throw herself at his head. Ruination or not have one or several sinful nights in his arms if she could. The very idea of him touching her, pulling her close, teasing her with his wicked mouth and unscrupulous words made her yearn to do just that.

Her lips twitched at the thought.

"Miss Hall, why are you grinning? Is my Latin wrong? Are you laughing at me?" Lady Alice questioned, her eyes wide with alarm.

"Oh no, not at all," Reign said, hugging the little girl quickly to stop the tears that she saw were on the verge of breaking over her sweet cheeks. "I merely cannot believe how well you're doing at such a young age. You'll be proficient with your Latin, too, in no time."

Lady Alice grinned too, happy again before she continued.

Reign tried to concentrate, but she could not help but wonder when her small cottage in Grafton would sell, and she would come into the funds. His lordship's gift was more significant than he knew, and it would change her life for the better, she hoped.

"Oh, Miss Hall, can you smell that?" Lady Alice said, sniffing the air like a hound.

Reign could not decipher anything out of the ordinary. "No, what is it that you smell?" she asked.

"I think cook is making honey cakes. May I go down to the kitchens? I always know when she's cooking them as the smell comes up through the servant stairs. Please, Miss Hall.

Pretty please," the little girl said, jumping up and down on the spot.

Reign closed the book of Latin and nodded. "Of course, you may. I will be in the music room when you've finished your afternoon tea, and we shall commence your music lesson to finish out today's lessons."

"Oh, thank you," the little girl squealed and was gone.

Reign packed up the schoolroom and walked to the window, staring out over the great estate. She could not push aside what his lordship had said to her last evening.

Did he believe her to be so far beneath him now, a governess, that she was unsuitable for such a lofty marriage? The knowledge stung but also shamed him in turn.

How high and mighty must one be to believe such things? In truth, she was no lower on the social ladder than when she had her Season. Certainly, she was just as poor, as her parents had left a trail of debt when they had left the city. She was a gentleman's daughter and still was, even if she had to earn her way through the world now. With his lordship paying off her family's debts, she was better off now more than ever.

She shook her head, hating the thought that by courting her, marrying her, he would cause strife and scandal to sully the Lupton-Gage name as he suggested. He could choose to fight to have her accepted, dismiss those who would mention her fall from financial grace if she ever had any to begin with, and marry her anyway.

But it seems she was wrong in that estimation, for he would not, not after all the trouble and scandal that the late Marchioness of Lupton-Gage had put the family through, anything resembling shame would be dismissed.

She would be dismissed ...

"Ah, there you are, Miss Hall. I wish to discuss with you the arrangements for the bedrooms with the houseguests arriving for the house party. We shall have to move you, I'm afraid," Mrs. Watkins said from the door, folding her hands before her. Reign ignored the glee that she could see burning in the old retainer's eyes, something she had noticed the moment his lordship had mentioned their connection in London.

"Of course, Mrs. Watkins. I shall pack my things now so the maids can come in and clean and prepare."

"Thank you, that will be most welcome."

Reign ignored the older woman's presence when she entered her room and went about collecting the few meager items she owned. A few books, letters from friends, and her clothes, which did not total many.

To save money and keep food in her belly, she had sold the gowns made for her in London and only kept one afternoon dress. How sad it was that the one gown she retained was once the height of fashion and beauty, and now looked no better than a servant's gown.

Tattered and torn, like her life.

She lifted her small valise and followed Mrs. Watkins out of the room and toward the servants' stairs. They went up another floor toward a long passage before a second passage came into view. "This is where the servants sleep, those who work upstairs in any case. Each room has a lock. Here is your key," she said, handing her a long, metal key hanging from a piece of string. "Room two, Miss Hall. Do let me know if you need extra blankets. The rooms are terribly cold at night this time of year."

Reign stood in the passage and watched as Mrs. Watkins strode away, her chin high, and a triumphant look upon her aged features. Turning on her heel, she walked the long corridor, taking note of the door numbers until she found two.

She entered the small space. An unlit fire sat against one wall, and a single bed with a rough metal frame on the other. A small, wooden chest and a bedside cabinet made up the remainder of the furniture. No chair before the fire, but she supposed she could always sit on the floor.

Reign dropped her valise and made her way over to the window. It was so very high up, and the view was the same one from the schoolroom downstairs, but merely two floors higher up. There were no curtains, not that it mattered, she supposed. No one would be climbing onto the roof to spy on her.

Well, at least she would not have to be in this room for long, not with her plans well on the way again. She turned about and went to her bag, unpacking her items and setting up her room for the night. Thankfully a tinderbox and flint sat beside a candle, along with a small pile of wood. They had not left her completely without comfort, it seemed.

And being this high up in the house, when his lordship hosted his house party, there was no reason why she would run into the guests and have to explain how she was once part of their world and why she no longer was.

Which, if after what Lord Lupton-Gage stated last evening, would be for the best, especially if those in attendance were known to her and knew of her Season in town.

With or without succumbing to her charms, a scandal may break in any case, merely by her being in the house with a gentleman who once paid court to her. She would prefer that not to happen, and she did not want to leave before she was able. Nor did she wish to be the reason Lady Alice was marred by scandal when she came of age. She would leave that up to the late Lady Lupton-Gage, who seemed to have that in hand.

SEVEN

The following days leading up to the house party ensured the estate was a hive of activity. The servants were busy polishing anything and everything that required a buffing cloth. Chandeliers were lowered and dusted. Fires were laid in all the guest bedrooms along with clean linens, and the dust cloths laid over furniture in unused rooms were removed.

Reign had found out during one of the servants' dinners that the marquess had not held a house party here since before his marriage and the word below stairs was that his lordship was only doing so to capture a new bride. A new mother for his motherless daughter.

That Mrs. Watkins had watched her most curiously during the conversation left Reign uncomfortable. Did the housekeeper believe she was after the position of wife and mother? That their shared history in London meant there had been something between them?

Maybe that was the case, but the housekeeper did not know their history, and Reign was determined to keep it that way.

Not that any of the servants ought to worry about her being the next Marchioness of Lupton-Gage. After his lordship's words to her two weeks past, he would not seek her to fill the position. As a governess, she was too far beneath his social rank now to be considered appropriate for such a lofty title.

Pain settled in her chest at the thought that she was left with this situation in life through no fault of her own.

"You will keep to your room at all times except for your lessons and meals, Miss Hall," Mrs. Watkins said as Reign stood beside the stove in the kitchen, enjoying a cup of tea with the cook.

"Of course," Reign replied, wishing she could gain the housekeeper's trust and friendship, but the old retainer seemed determined to dislike her more and more each day.

"His lordship will be busy with his guests and ensuring their entertainment and needs are met. Any discussions you are required to have with his lordship will need to take place after the house party. It is only a week. I'm sure anything you need to know is not so important that you must harass his lordship," Mrs. Watkins stated bluntly before turning up her nose and walking from the kitchen, the many keys that hung from her waist clanging about with each step.

"Well, I never. What have you done to Mrs. Watkins to be so disliked, lass? She is very sharp with you, if I may say so myself," the cook said as she went on with her tasks for tonight's dinner.

Reign frowned after Mrs. Watkins, knowing all too well what she had done to the woman, not that it was her shortcoming. "I think she believes I'm going to try to win the heart of the marquess," she blurted to the cook, unable to hide her thoughts a moment longer.

The cook whistled, studying her in a new light. "And are you, lass? You're certainly pretty enough to turn any man's head. Why even young Marcus in the stables had mentioned how pretty and sharp you are."

Reign smiled, but she did not need those kinds of compliments. It was one of the reasons why the housekeeper refused to be friendly. "I'm saving all the money I can so I may leave England. It has not been kind to me these past several years and I need a fresh start. Nothing is keeping me here in England, and no marquess wishes to marry me. I do not know why Mrs. Watkins has to be so unkind. How am I to stay in my room during the day when I have my free time? I shall like to stroll outside, but am I not allowed? I will be housebound for a week, and that in itself is unbearable."

"Of course you can stroll, Miss Hall. Do not heed what the housekeeper states. She is not the boss of you, not really," the cook said, picking up a spoon to stir a large bowl of soup. "His lordship is since you are his daughter's governess."

Reign sighed, taking her cup to the sink and rinsing it. She did not want to cause trouble or concern for the housekeeper. "I suppose it is only a week. I shall survive being in my room for a little while. I will ask his lordship for more books to keep me occupied."

The cook shrugged but glanced at her, disappointment shining in her weary eyes. "As you wish, Miss Hall, but I know for certain that I should not be locking myself away just to please Mrs. Watkins. Why she ought to be ashamed of herself for even suggesting such a thing to you."

"I'm new here. I do not want to cause trouble." She laid her cup on the drying rack. "I shall see you tomorrow at breakfast," she said, starting upstairs.

The house was eerily quiet after a day of nothing but noise as she climbed the stairs. Without thinking, she exited on the floor that once housed her room. She hesitated in the center of the passageway before turning on her heel and starting for the staircase again.

"Miss Hall?" a familiar, deep baritone said from the direction of the stairs.

Reign cringed, not wishing to meet his lordship alone and practically in the dark. She schooled her features and turned. The moment she did, she wished she had not.

Lord Lupton-Gage was not properly attired. His cravat hung about his neck, his shirt pulled free from his breeches, and he wore no shoes.

Possibly the reason she had not heard him before he spoke.

"My lord," she said, clasping her hands before her and praying for strength. For all of Mrs. Watkins rules and management, there was a grain of truth to her concerns.

Reign and the marquess had a history, and the last thing she needed to do was to repeat that narrative. But seeing him now, dressed as he was, disheveled and as handsome as ever, well, keeping from seducing the man would be a triumph in which she must succeed.

UPON SEEING HER IN THE PASSAGE, Bellamy had taken a moment to drink in the sight of Reign. Would it always be like this, he wondered. This craving to be with her, to kiss her sweet lips, if even for one more delicious time.

He strolled up to Miss Hall and frowned. "Have you forgotten something downstairs? Why were you heading back toward the servants' stairs?" he asked, looking past her to see if someone else was lurking in the shadows of his home. A manservant, perhaps, wanting to court Miss Hall.

He pushed the thought out of his mind. Even if that were true, none of those particulars were his business. Not unless they married or his daughter's governess became pregnant.

He ground his teeth, an uncomfortable sensation running down his spine at that offensive thought.

"I forgot where my room was, my lord. I apologize and bid you goodnight," she said, turning on her heel to flee from his presence.

Without thought, he reached out and clasped her hand, pulling her to stop. "Miss Hall, you sleep on this floor beside my daughter's room. What are you talking about?" he asked.

She bit her lip, a frown marring her normally perfect brow. "Well, as to that," she hedged, looking around as if someone could be listening in on their conversation. "I've moved, my lord. I thought it best considering the house party. May I speak frankly?" she asked him.

He nodded, needing to hear what she had to say. "Of course."

"Well," she paused, "servants are normally either below stairs or above the family's rooms. It was not right for me to be on this level, and I have since moved upstairs. But I can assure you that I shall not shirk my duties. Lady Alice will have the continued care and lessons we have had so far, my lord."

Bellamy shook his head. The notion that she had moved due to discomfort did not sit well with him. "I hope it has nothing to do with our conversation the other evening, Miss Hall. I did not mean to make you feel unwelcome. I just thought we needed to discuss the matter before too many weeks passed with you working here," he said.

"No, nothing of the kind," she assured him, waving his concerns aside. "It is for the best, which I'm sure you agree."

Bellamy was not so sure about that fact. He appreciated that she was close to his daughter's room in case of an emergency. Not to mention he liked that she was close to him.

He shook the thought aside. She was not for him. He had told her so himself. He could not keep torturing himself back and forth as to why he did not care that she was a governess. He must think of his daughter in this regard.

He ran a hand over his jaw, debating the matter and wondering if Mrs. Watkins had something to do with Reign's move. The housekeeper did not seem overly warm to her, and if her obvious dislike continued, he would be forced to say something.

"Very well," he conceded. If she truly thought it acceptable, then he would not stop her. It was probably for the best in any case since he had a terribly hard time concentrating on anything when Miss Hall was near. Sleeping included.

"The house looks marvelous for the guests, my lord. They start to arrive tomorrow, I understand?" She pulled her arm out of his hold, which to his horror, he still held.

Dear Lord, how much wine did he consume this evening at dinner not to have realized he held her near him after several minutes?

You like holding her. You want to embrace her again.

And that was the rub. Not that either of them would act upon it, not after their conversation a fortnight ago.

His daughter deserved a steady, uncomplicated life and did not need her name sullied by scandal. As it was, she would be associated forever with her mother, the woman who left them both to travel the world with her lover. A woman who left countless debts across Europe for him to remedy when the accounts and letters of demand arrived.

He could not satisfy the growing lust, the affection he once harbored for Miss Hall, now his daughter's governess.

She stared at him, her eyes large blue pools

that reminded him of a deep loch in Scotland he once admired.

"The house is prepared for the guests, I'm told. Some of whom you're associated with," he said, wanting to please her even when he should not.

"Once were associated with, my lord. My circumstances in life do impose limits on me and whom I can speak to," she said, reminding him of how he must have sounded when he placed the unspoken line between their social spheres.

High and mighty. Dismissive and warning her away. How she must detest him now.

He needed to stop pining for the woman before him, but blast it all to hell, he could not. Even now, when he knew better, when he had declared the rules verbally that they must both adhere to, he wanted to reach for her. Remind her of how well they fit together.

Just as they had that one long-forgotten night in London.

Eight

Reign felt as though she was trapped. Caught between desire and denial. She shouldn't want the man who stood before her in a dark, quiet passageway of his ancestral home, and yet she could not force her feet to move either.

They refused to heed what her mind was screaming at her.

Leave. Run. Return to her room before she succumbed to his charms for a second time.

She needed this employment to ensure her survival and plans to come to fruition. To throw herself at him, to take what she wanted was madness. Worse, she did want him. Desperately so. She longed for every part of him. To kiss and revel in the feel of his hunger. The very thought of it left her breathless and she fisted her hands at her sides, forcing herself to stop. To think.

"Please do not look at me like that, my lord. It is not fair," she pleaded. And it was not proper.

So much of her life had been taken from her, her hopes and dreams.

She had moved to the Lake District determined to take the first step of many to her new life, only to arrive at a destination that threw her back into the predicament she found herself years ago.

"How am I looking at you?" he asked, his voice a seductive purr that made her question her morals. He stepped closer still, towering over her. She had little doubt he knew what he was doing. How he was making it near impossible for her to deny him. To deny them both.

Her stomach clenched, and she raised her chin, determined not to fall.

Do not slip, Reign. Everything depends on you keeping your head and your heart ...

"As if you wish to kiss me," she breathed, the breath in her lungs tight, making speech difficult. In fact, being this close to the marquess had always had this effect on her.

Blasted, a disgustingly good-looking man that he was.

"And if I did, would you kiss me back?" He clasped one of her hands and slipped it into his. His palm was soft, his fingers long and strong as they wrapped about hers, holding her close.

"You warned me away but a fortnight ago,

and I can smell the scent of whisky on your breath. Please do not say one thing when you have your wits and slide into this character when you do not. It is beneath you," she said, needing to chastise him, if it meant that he would stop talking to her in such a way.

Stop taunting her with a life that was not hers to live.

Not anymore.

Her words seemed to pull him out of the trance he was living in, and he stepped back, dropping her hand. "You are right, of course. My apologies, Reign," he stated, using her given name when he should not. "I knew it would be hard to live here under this roof with you and not come across you at different times of day and night and fall back into the easy conversation we had when we were in London. I forget that you're a governess when I see you about."

And beneath his notice, she understood, watching him. He ran a hand through his already unruly hair. "I wish you a good night," he stated, walking past her toward his room.

Reign watched him, ensured he made his chamber without incident, and then returned to the servants' stairs. Making her own floor, she stepped into the passageway and skidded to a halt at the sight of Mrs. Watkins, hands clasped before her and a scowl on her already displeased visage.

"Miss Hall, it is against the household rules to

be out and about this late at night. And then you were just downstairs with his lordship when I explicitly told you to keep away from him. He will not marry you or court you, no matter your history. You are a governess now if I need remind you," she said, her lips pulling into a tight, dissatisfied line. "No longer the belle of the ball."

"I apologize, Mrs. Watkins. It was not purposefully done. It will not happen again," she promised, hoping that it would not. For if she came across Lord Lupton-Gage again, she was not so sure she would be able to deny herself a taste of him. A taste of the past, now lost to her forever, whether his lordship was foxed or sober.

"See that it does not," she declared, pushing past her and knocking into her shoulder.

Reign clasped her arm and stood in the passage momentarily, wondering if the housekeeper had just assaulted her. She had never been pushed against by another person in such a manner. Nor did she like the thought that Mrs. Watkins anger could turn physical if she kept finding her in locations and conversations she did not agree with.

She would have to be extra careful to avoid everyone the marquess invited to the house party and his lordship himself. She required this position to last for as long as she needed it to. There was no other option for her than to try to make the best of this bad situation.

* * *

BELLAMY WOKE LATE THE NEXT MORNING, his head thumping and a sharp pain that would not relent at the back of his skull, knocking against his head like a bell. He reached behind and did not feel any protruding lump as if he had hit his head.

He glanced at his bedside table and spied two bottles of whisky. What had he managed last evening, and why was he drinking?

He groaned and slumped back onto his pillows, staring up at the ceiling, knowing full well what his issue was.

Miss Reign Hall. Situated in the attic upstairs, a few mere steps and doors from him. She would be awake by now, of course, dressed and possibly already having given his daughter her lessons for the day.

She would not lie about all morning after a night of drinking.

He pushed back his bedding, and his valet appeared within a moment of his feet hitting the Aubusson rug.

"My lord, a bath?" Chambers suggested.

He nodded. "Yes, I think that is best. The guests arrive late this afternoon, and I need to get my equilibrium back by then and remove this headache."

"I shall fetch a tisane, my lord," his valet said before leaving the room to order the water and tisane.

Bellamy soaked for as long as he could before the water became too cold for comfort and then dressed and readied himself for the day. By the time he strolled downstairs, he was feeling much improved, although he could not remember a blasted thing that had happened the evening before.

A faint recollection of Miss Hall floated in his mind, but he could not remember what they had spoken of. If they had spoken at all ...

Laughter caught his attention, and he walked to the window, looking out over the front courtyard to see Miss Hall and Alice starting down the long, maple tree-lined drive. Both wore bonnets, and Alice held Miss Hall's hand, swinging their arms merrily as they chattered about whatever they were discussing.

He sighed, appreciating the picture they made and wishing his life, or at least Miss Hall's life, had not traveled the path it had.

One of the reasons why he had invited his good friends Lord and Lady Chilsten to the house party this week. If anyone could change Miss Hall's thoughts on being a governess before it was too late, it was the Marchioness of Chilsten.

A carriage appeared on the drive, and he sighed, knowing that it would only be a matter of time before the house was full of guests and he would not be able to dwell each day on Miss

Hall, who unfortunately occupied a lot of his mind.

A knock sounded on the door, and his butler announced the first of the guests.

Over the next several hours, carriage after carriage arrived, and he greeted each and every guest in the foyer, welcoming them to his home. Most were from the Lake District; few were from London, other than the Marquess and Marchioness of Chilsten.

He had not thought they would attend, but when he had mentioned who had arrived on his doorstep for work, the marchioness had written him back, announcing they would be in attendance.

He did not see Miss Hall for the remainder of the day, not even when he went upstairs to wish his daughter goodnight.

He left Alice's room and couldn't help but wonder why the housekeeper was there instead of the nanny. It was, after all, the nanny and Miss Hall's employment to care for his child. The idea that the housekeeper was wary of Miss Hall was now even more prevalent in his mind.

"Ahh here you are," a familiar and much-longed-for voice shouted from the foyer.

Bellamy glanced down the stairs and chuckled at seeing his friend and his beautiful wife, the Marquess and Marchioness of Chilsten.

He came down to greet them, hugging the

marquess and kissing the marchioness on the cheek. "You made it. I hope your journey was not too arduous."

The marchioness scoffed, pulling off her gloves and bonnet. "Well, of course it was arduous. You live almost in Scotland, Lord Lupton-Gage," she teased him, grinning.

He chuckled, clapping the marquess on the back. "Come, we shall have drinks in my study. The remainder of the guests are resting in their rooms until dinner."

"That sounds most needed," Chilsten said, taking his wife's hand and pulling her with him.

They made their way into the library, his guests seating themselves before the fire on the settee, both of them sighing in relief. No doubt more than pleased they were no longer in a jarring carriage.

Bellamy rang for tea and joined them. "Thank you for coming. I know it's an awfully long journey for a house party, but I need your help."

The marchioness leaned forward, meeting his eyes. "How long has Reign been working here? I should imagine it is vastly odd, considering before your marriage to Lady Sally, there was talk in town of your considerable interest in Miss Hall. That she is now your daughter's governess must be a little disconcerting," the marchioness stated.

That was an understatement. He was not

only disconcerted by her being here but also downright floundering with his morals. "She is determined to leave England, as you may already know, but I do not like the idea. She is not a woman of the world. I fear for her safety while on the ship and abroad. Am I wrong in this concern?" Bellamy asked.

The marquess glanced at his wife before turning to him. "Depends if you're concerned because you still feel something for Miss Hall or if it is merely because, as you say, she is a woman."

The marchioness scoffed, "I think it is because you had always wanted to marry her and were denied that right when the scandal of you and Lady Sally broke in London. Tell me," she pinned him with an unflinching stare, "why can you not merely ask Reign to marry you? What is stopping you?"

He sighed, shaking his head and wishing his life could be different. "You know the late Marchioness of Lupton-Gage lived a scandalous life. She did not care for the daughter we made, nor what her actions abroad with her lover caused back in England. The more scandal, the better, from what I have been told. But I cannot allow such tarnish to continue against my name. My daughter deserves better. If I then go and marry her governess, how does that look? It makes me appear like a nefarious landlord who beds his servants, and I cannot do that to Alice. My concern is, even if she does return to London with you, how many people know she's been in employment here? I think the scandal would be too great, and I must relent and let her go."

The marchioness shook her head, watching him, and he did not particularly like how she studied him. "We can fix this, my lord. Be patient. I'm here now, and I shall not fail my friend. I shall convince her to come to London with me," she declared.

Bellamy nodded, but something deep within him knew it was likely already too late.

NINE

Reign remained in her room as instructed and watched the outdoor games that were being played the following morning. She could not recognize any of the guests, which she supposed was a good thing, and she had traveled downstairs early this morning to complete Lady Alice's lessons before the guests were out of bed.

Mrs. Watkins seemed pleased by her absence from the main part of the house and had even bestowed a kind word to her at lunch.

A knock sounded on her door, and she strode over to it, opening it to find her closest friend staring back at her.

"Julia?" she gasped as they moved and pulled each other into an embrace. "What are you doing here? You are a long way from home this far north," she said.

Julia chuckled, pulling back, a warm, wistful

smile on her face. "I'm here for the house party, and Lord Lupton-Gage informed me you're a governess here. How did that occur? I never thought when you suggested that you would work for a living that you would find employment at the very gentleman's home whom you once coveted."

Reign glanced down the hall, glad to see no one was about and pulled Julia into her room. "Come inside and sit. The housekeeper here abhors me, and if she sees me conversing with a houseguest, she'll have my hide scolded."

Alarmed, Julia followed her into the room. The shock on her friend's features when she glanced about her bedroom, at the plainness of the bed and furniture, the small fire one had to sit upon to keep warm, shamed her.

"It is not much," Reign said, feeling as though she needed to defend her pitiful space. "But it is all I need for the moment. You know my plans, and I do not have long before I can leave and let his lordship be free of me."

"He wrote me," Julia disclosed. "Invited us to the house party with the hopes that I would attend and talk you into traveling back with me to London. You know that I'm wealthy enough to keep you until you marry. There is no reason why you need to stay here." Julia clasped her hand. "You're my oldest friend. Let me do this for you, Reign."

Reign sighed, coming to sit beside her oldest and most loyal friend on her bed. The only place to sit, unfortunately. "Thank you for the offer, but it is still no. Not only because that is too generous, but because there is a little girl who needs stability. I'm a governess now, and I need to ensure that I teach her and care for her for as long as I have until a new governess can be found to replace me. I will not abandon her. Not after her mother has done exactly that."

"You care for the child," Julia stated. It was not a question. "And what about her father? How did you not know if it was his lordship's estate when you wrote regarding the position?"

Reign disclosed what she knew of the position before traveling to Derbyshire and her shock when she was introduced to Lord Lupton-Gage in the corridor downstairs.

"Well, do not say that I did not try to change your mind, and it's admirable that you wish to remain here to teach before leaving. But America, Reign? Are you not scared? Can you not stay in England?"

She shrugged, knowing there was no other option for her. Not unless she miraculously inherited thousands of pounds. This was her lot in life. She would not be a burden to anyone, and certainly not her friend, who had a family to care for and a husband to keep.

"I will be fine and shall write as I promised.

But his lordship has made it clear that I'm beneath his notice, and this is for the best."

"He has said such a thing to you?" Julia demanded.

"Yes," she said, wishing he had not. His words had stung the last vestiges of pride she held of her old life as his equal. "I'm a governess, one step up from a servant. I can see his point as much as it pains me. I can only hope the others attending the house party do not know who I am."

Julia narrowed her eyes in thought, looking out toward her small window. "I do not believe anyone is here from London, but that does not mean they do not have relatives or were, in fact, in Town when we had our debuts. You must prepare yourself to be noticed and think upon what you will say when that occurs." Julia paused, taking her hand and squeezing. "But please think upon my offer. As my oldest friend, please do that, at least. I beseech you."

Reign smiled, nodding. "Very well, I shall think upon it and give you my answer before you leave."

BELLAMY KICKED HIS HORSE AND RODE hard into the copse of trees that surrounded his estate, needing to get out, to have some quiet while his house all but buckled at the many guests he had invited.

A mistake he could not wait to end. Five more days and he would be free of the endless chatter, the constant flirtatious glances from certain unattached ladies, and the ever-increasing missing governess who had avoided his presence since his guests had arrived.

He jumped a small hedge grove, landing in a puddle of mud. The dirty water splashed up over his Hession boots and tan breeches, but he did not care. His mind was focused elsewhere.

Where it ought not to be ...

He wrenched his horse to a stop when he came to a part of the river some distance from his house, a place where he had swum often as a boy.

It did not take him long to strip down to his breeches, kicking off his boots and stockings, before diving into the refreshingly cold water.

He came up for air, running a hand through his hair, and felt the breath in his lungs seize.

"Miss Hall? What in the zounds are you doing here?" Bellamy went to cover his cock and then realized it was not him who ought to be concerned with propriety.

Miss Hall was the woman. Should she not be concerned?

He winced at the thought. Well, she ought to be troubled that he may ogle her at every chance he received. Blasted rogue he was starting to think like.

"My lord, I could ask you the same question.

Today, as per Mrs. Watkins's roster, is my day off, and I thought I would escape the house and heat and come for a swim. One of the stablemen told me of this place, and I was curious," she defended.

Bellamy swallowed, noting she did not try to cover the front of herself, her shift all but transparent in the water. Not that he could see her as perfectly as he wished, but if he moved closer ...

Damn it all to hell. What was he thinking? He could not do that.

Could he?

No. He ground his jaw, praying for sainthood.

"What stableman was that?" he demanded to know, hating the biting jealousy that raged through him at the thought of Reign being courted by a groom or one of his drivers. Not that she could not do as she wished, she was beholden to no one, but still, the thought left a bitter taste in his mouth, and he did not like to imagine such things.

"What does it matter which stableman told me of this place?" She scoffed at his question, staring at him in astonishment. "What an absurd question to ask me, my lord," she said, taking a cautionary step toward the bank of the river and halting when her action left more of her upper body open for him to see.

"I do not like my servants cavorting about

with each other. It leads to unplanned children and hasty weddings and leaves my household looking for more servants to replace them." The instant he said the words, he wished he could rip them back.

She was no servant, no matter how much she pretended to be. The circumstances of her life may have placed her in this position, but it was not who she was. He ought to be whipped for making her face crumple with the hurt he inflicted.

"I'll be sure not to sleep with the groom then, my lord. If it will please the esteemed Lord Lupton-Gage," she spat back at him, her eyes no longer fearful of her wet gown or him seeing her thus, but burning with an anger he had placed there.

She moved toward the bank, heedless that when she stepped up onto the grass, her shift was as transparent as he feared, leaving her bottom easy to admire.

She picked up her gown and hastily threw it over her shift, heedless of how wet she remained. "You have a lot of nerve," she growled at him, slipping on her boots before she turned to look at him. "I'm here, doing the best that I can under the circumstances of my life and our history, and yet you taunt me, ridicule me as if I'm some lightskirt who'll be easily swayed by the first man who speaks to me that is not you. Do not fear that I shall fall under the spell of anyone male at this estate. I have decided that your sex is detestable, and you are too, just to be clear."

Bellamy watched her but did not reply. He deserved the remark. Hell, he deserved so much more than that tongue-lashing. He knew what he was doing, being a jealous cur because someone else may have something that he had wanted and lost.

And now she was lost forever due to the unfairness of her life. "Please return to London with Lady Chilsten. You will be safe from the perils of America, and I shall sleep better knowing ..."

"That I'm not under the same roof as you?" She chuckled, picking up a small basket he had not noticed before. Had she picnicked here?

"You should marry again, my lord. Mayhap if you do, my presence here would not upset you so very much," she said before leaving him alone.

Bellamy punched the water, which did little but splash into his face. He rolled his eyes, staring at the sky and praying for some sensible thought. But he knew it would not come. Not with Miss Hall under his roof. He could never think straight when she was around; even after all these years, that dilemma had not altered.

TEN

Reign knew she was acting like an awful person, but she could not help herself. Lord Lupton-Gage deserved everything he received after their conversation the previous day at the river.

He was jealous. That was as clear as the water in which they swam, but to talk down to her, tell her who she ought to speak to, and warn her against being a light-skirt, well, she would not stand for it.

She had not arrived at his estate on purpose, and nor would she allow him to believe his telling her off, warning her away from young Marcus— as if she would fall at the young stableman's feet because the marquess was no longer interested— was an insult.

In truth, she had sworn off all men and would never marry. If she found a position in America that kept her safe and paid well, there was no reason why she would look for a keeper, especially if that keeper were a jealous cur like his lordship.

She strolled into the back gardens and looked over to the stables, waving to Marcus, who held a horse's hoof while cleaning out the muck. He smiled at her and waved back before she continued to walk toward a pretty hedged garden that she had not inspected before.

When she reached the secluded part of the park, she found the hedge was much higher than she first thought, well above one story, and dense. She supposed it was very old from the looks of it.

She walked through a small gate cut into the hedge and found a sinking garden in a rectangular shape. Stone steps led down to a central pond of the same shape, and the beauty of the oasis left her speechless.

Tomorrow she would bring Lady Alice here for her lessons instead of the schoolroom. It seemed no one in attendance of the house party had found the hidden garden, and she hoped it would stay that way.

"Good afternoon, Miss Hall," a voice she had not expected to hear here said from behind. She turned and found Marcus standing inside the gate, his hat twisted between his hands.

"Good afternoon, Marcus. I hope your day is going well," she said, unsure why the groom had come to speak to her and not liking how nervous he was about the fact.

"I wanted to come to talk to you, to explain that helping you find the river the other day did not mean anything. I have a sweetheart, you see. I love her and will marry her, so I didn't want you to think that I would do her wrong."

Reign held up her hand, halting his words. Mortification swamped her, and anger, not at Marcus but at one nosy marquess, filled her blood.

"I never thought anything of the kind, and I would appreciate you telling me who put these doubts and thoughts into your head," she demanded, knowing exactly who had warned the groom off and embarrassed everyone involved in the interim.

Marcus cringed, glancing over his shoulder. "I would prefer not to say, miss, but I do hope we can be friends, Miss Hall."

Reign sighed and prayed for patience. She would murder Lord Lupton-Gage when she saw him next. "We were always friends, Marcus, and nothing more. Please do not dwell on the idea that I fancied you. I did not. I only ever wished for a friend, no more than that."

Relief poured from the young man, and her determination to eradicate his lordship grew.

"Well, I'm relieved to hear that, Miss Hall. I

wish you a pleasant afternoon," he said before leaving her alone in the garden.

She closed her eyes a moment, thinking of what she would use to knock his lordship over his thick skull. Without further thought, she stormed from the gardens and headed straight for the house. Thankfully most of the guests were on the side lawn playing various games, and the house remained eerily quiet.

Reign came across Chambers, his lordship's valet, coming out of the library. "Chambers, is his lordship in?" she asked, striding toward the door.

"He is, Miss Hall, but he is not available at present," he said.

Reign ignored him and continued entering the room and finding Lord Lupton-Gage behind his desk. The sight of him caught her off guard, and she steeled herself to remain angry and not ogle the handsome monster.

He held a quill, and he quickly scribbled on parchment. The shirt he wore rolled partway up, revealing strong, muscular arms that had once lovingly held her.

She longed to be held by them still, if she were truthful.

Annoying cad.

She shut the door and locked it before striding over to the desk. He leaned back in his chair, watching her, and she narrowed her eyes.

Did the fiend know why she was angry and expected her?

She leaned on the desk and tried to tower over him but knew with the several feet of mahogany that separated them, it was unlikely to work.

"So now you're warning off the servants from courting me? How dare you when I liked Marcus too," she lied, pinning him to his chair with a steely gaze. Or at least her best attempt at one.

"So you did fancy the groom. I knew it," he stated, leaning back in his chair and glaring. "As I said, such relationships under my roof are prohibited."

Reign would later wonder what came over her, but having had enough of his detachment and seeming jealousy, she wanted to test him, to prove how much he was fibbing to himself.

She stormed about the desk, leaned down, and kissed him.

Hard.

He stilled before reaching for her. His hands slipped about her face, running into her hair as his mouth turned the kiss into much more than the punishment she had intended.

He stood, and she felt her bottom press against the desk before he hoisted her atop it. Papers and quills fell to the floor as he savaged her mouth in a kiss that left her reeling.

Somewhere along the road to punish him,

she had awoken a fire in him that burned out of control. Their tongues tangled and pins fell from her hair. His hands cupped her face with such care, and yet there was no modesty, no sensitivity to this kiss.

It was wild, wicked, and utterly captivating.

And it was over as quickly as it had started.

He wrenched from her, his hand coming to his lips as if she had assaulted him somehow, and she supposed in a fashion she had.

"You should leave," he commanded, pointing to the door. "Before anyone sees us."

His words spiked her anger, and she clasped the lapels of his coat, pulling him close, going nose to nose with the marquess. "If you do not want me, if I'm no longer good enough for your aristocratic blood, then you do not get to choose whom I speak to and whom I choose to have in my life. I may be a governess now, but that does not mean that you can treat me with so little respect." She shook her head, glad that he did not refute her claims. "Had you just asked, you would have known that Marcus has a sweetheart, and I never turned his head before you warned him away from me, making a fool of everyone, including yourself."

Reign slipped from the desk and strode to the door, needing to leave before she did anything else stupid, like kiss the shocked, enticing look off his lordship's good-looking face.

. . .

BELLAMY NEEDED A DISTRACTION AND A WIFE, a caring, loving mother for his daughter. Or at least that is what he told himself when he sat with Lady Miller after dinner in the drawing room, determined to listen to her recount her Season with precise, long, drawn-out detail while Lady Chilsten played the piano.

He glanced across the room and narrowed his eyes at Lord Chilsten's amused smirk, who had noticed his attention toward the Earl of Miller's widow.

He inwardly swore. What was he going to do? What *was* he doing was more to the question.

That damn kiss had near buckled him to his knees to the point he was on the verge of asking her to be his wife. Immediately. As in within the next few hours.

Bloody hell, he was doomed. He did not need another wife who would bring nothing but scandal to his door. Not that she would convey the same kind of scandal as his wife had, but even so, to marry one's servant was not what one ought to do.

His good friend, currently smirking at him, ought to know better than anyone of that fact since he did indeed marry his maid and paid a hefty price for it.

Thankfully after some time, the *ton* and his now wife had forgiven him, but he was not so sure the *ton* would be so kind to him. The late Lady Lupton-Gage had returned to London after the birth of their child and had promptly had multiple affairs with numerous married men. The ladies of the *ton* had long memories, and he doubted they would forgive him for not being able to keep his wife in line and out of their husband's beds.

As for Miss Hall, she was impoverished and had no sisters who had married titled men of influence in Town to welcome their brother-in-law back into the fold as Lord Chilsten had.

Miss Hall was a governess, a servant who had fallen on hard times. Society would think she had married him for position and safety. They would be the talk of the town, much like he was when married to Sally.

He shook his head, frowning. No. He could not do that to Alice. She deserved a renewed, unsullied, and uncomplicated Season in Town after a messy childhood.

"Lord Lupton-Gage, have I said something you do not agree with? You're shaking your head," Lady Miller said, concern shadowing her large, brown eyes.

"No, nothing of the kind. I was merely stretching my neck, and I think I may have pulled a muscle," he said, wondering if his excuse sounded as lame as it was.

"Correct me if I'm wrong," she said, fluttering her eyelashes. "But did I see Miss Reign Hall earlier today in the gardens? Did she not debut with the Marchioness of Chilsten years ago?"

And here it was, the start of the rumors and scandal.

Bellamy fumbled for words before the truth, or at least a very cautious version of it, was said. "Ah, you did," he ventured. "She is accompanying Lady Chilsten but did not wish to attend the house party," he lied, wondering when he believed this version of the truth was any better than telling her ladyship that Reign was a governess to his daughter.

"How scandalous of her not to attend," she hedged. "Are we so disagreeable that she would not come and greet us all?" Lady Miller pursed her lips, watching him keenly. "Is she a simpleton?" her ladyship asked. "Does she no longer know how to go about in society? I know she had been absent for several years, and I suppose she may have lost the ability to converse with others."

Bellamy choked, sipping his whisky at the statement from Lady Miller. He cleared his throat, shaking his head. "She is not a simpleton, that I'm aware."

But after their kiss this afternoon, he feared

he might be one. She had left him reeling, and blast the roguish ways he had wanted to continue the kiss. Had wanted to feel every little ounce of her body, rake his hands through her long, brown locks, and kiss her until he could not imagine kissing anyone else ever again.

Not that he did not already think such, much to his demise.

Eleven

Thankfully the following day, Reign was able to avoid Lord Lupton-Gage. She spent the day teaching Lady Alice in the secluded garden before watching her riding lesson before dinner.

The day passed quickly, and only every so often she caught glimpses of the house guests, who seemed to have left the estate today for an excursion or picnic if the large baskets of food indicated their goals.

She sat beside Lady Alice, reading her a bedtime story the little girl asked for often. Her eyelids dipped and eventually closed, but Reign continued for another five minutes before blowing out the candle beside her bed and pulling up her blankets.

She turned to leave and jumped at the sight of Lord Lupton-Gage leaning against the doorway, watching her.

"I'm too late, it seems. I'll have to apologize to Alice tomorrow for not getting back in time to wish her goodnight. I had hoped to be back to read the story myself," he said.

Reign placed the book back on the shelf and moved toward the door, her escape that the marquess was currently blocking.

The closer she came to him, the more she could smell the hint of brandy on his breath. Was he foxed? Was that why he was being so relaxed even though any of his guests could come upon them at any time?

"She was very tired and fell asleep quickly. I do not think she was upset that she did not see you this evening," she said, stepping past him.

He clasped her hand and pulled her to a stop. Reign looked up and met his eyes, and her stomach clenched in the wicked, restless way that it always had when around the marquess.

He was her weakness. She had such high hopes during her Season that he would court her and marry her, and instead, he married someone else entirely. A rich, well-dowered woman of nobility who tricked him into gaining her a title.

Reign had never stood a chance. She wasn't devious enough to reign supreme in London.

His gaze burned with a need that she recognized, but ought to deny. "Please move, my lord. This does not help either of us," she pleaded. She should push past him. Demand he let her leave, but her feet would not move.

Her mind and heart at odds over the matter.

"I cannot get that kiss out of my head," he whispered, a pained expression on his face. His fingers slipped down her arm to link with hers. "I cannot seem to let you go."

For a moment, Reign tipped toward the verge of scandal. To leap into the unknown and his lordship's arms and let him show her just how far a kiss could carry a lady down the road of ruin.

But she did not.

"Goodnight, my lord," she said with more conviction than she felt before pushing past him and toward the servant's stairs. Her back burned, and she knew he watched her until she was out of sight.

The urge to run back to him was beyond her endurance, yet she persisted. He did not want to marry his servant. She was a walking scandal she did not want to bring onto his family, and she would never marry a man who would resent her should they be ostracized by the *ton* merely because he fell in love with a governess.

How soon would that love turn to spite and resentment?

No, she could never survive the marquess looking upon her with either of those emotions.

. . .

BELLAMY CLOSED HIS EYES AND FOUGHT the desire that burned through him. The need to go after her and slake both their passions. He glanced in the direction she had walked and debated going after her. She would not be far.

"What do you think you're doing?" a familiar voice said from the darkness of the passage.

He turned and found Chilsten watching him, one suspect brow raised in his direction.

Bellamy swore and strolled toward his friend. "I have no idea what I'm doing. I feel at sea when Miss Hall is in my presence, and unfortunately, she is in my company more often than not."

"Come, let us sit in the parlor and talk. There are many ears about this evening," Chilsten said, moving away from the guest suites.

Bellamy followed, hating that his inaction, his inability to do what he had promised himself, had been seen by another.

They entered the parlor, and thankfully the fire was alight and gave them ample light to pour two glasses of whisky. Chilsten handed him one, a concerned expression on his face.

"What is going on between you and Miss Hall? I know I viewed something just before, and as your friend, I'm not fearful of telling you that I'm troubled," he said.

Bellamy ran a hand through his hair, agitated himself that he would crumble and sleep with his daughter's governess. He cringed, hating to think of Miss Hall in such a way. Once, he viewed her as an equal, even with her lack of funds that so many other debutantes had in excess. He did not care about such things, for he had enough money for both of them. But now ... now she was working for him, and everything was different, wrong somehow.

"She is my daughter's governess, and yet, when I'm near her, I cannot help but want her. I want what I lost all those years ago when I married Sally."

Chilsten studied him as he sipped his drink. "Lady Lupton-Gage has passed, my friend. What does it matter if you marry a woman who isn't as high in society as so many worthless ones are?" he asked him. "You should not worry what people think so much. Or you will wake up one day, old and weary in your bed, and realize that you wasted your life on people who never mattered."

Bellamy nodded, his friend's words making more sense than anything he had thought of since the moment Miss Hall had come to be at his estate. He should not care what others thought, he knew that, but Sally had been so very wild. So much damage was done to his name. To his daughter's name.

"How can I put my daughter through such a scandal after all that her mother has done to her?" he argued.

Chilsten shrugged. "She's five. I do not think

she will remember what happens now, so long as she is loved and cared for."

Bellamy downed his brandy, relishing the burn the drink left down his throat. "To my shame, I wish my daughter's mother was Reign. I wish she were my marchioness. How can I remain a gentleman when all I want to do, every moment of every day, is be with her? I want to seduce her, have her in my bed, my life."

"Then society be damned. Take what you want, Gage. Marry her and make the both of you very happy," his friend urged.

Bellamy rubbed a hand over his jaw. Could he ignore all the rules and do what he wanted for the first time in his life? Gain what he had wanted for so long, and to hell with what the *ton* thought of his choice. He would never regret marrying Reign. How could he when she was utterly perfect? The kiss he had shared with her, a kiss that had rattled him and shown him everything that he had lost by making an error all those years ago in London.

"If I do as you advise and do as I want, there will be a scandal," he stated.

Chilsten nodded. "I know all too well what it is like to cause scandal. And as your friend who made a similar mistake in marrying the wrong woman before I married Julia, let me tell you that whatever you choose will be hard, a decision not to be taken lightly. But you have mine and Julia's support, whatever you decide to do." Chilsten paused, sipping his brandy. "Society knows you were deceived into entering that parlor with Lady Sally, and while they embraced the wedding, there is knowledge and understanding as to why you would marry Miss Hall now that you can."

Bellamy nodded, hope for the first time flickering to life in his mind. He had not thought to have to face such a choice. He did not expect to see Miss Hall again, certainly not under his roof.

Had he come across her in London in passing, he knew he could deny the pull she had always had on him, but here, in his home, running into her in the middle of the night when she was reading his daughter a bedtime story, well, that was another matter entirely.

"Thank you, Chilsten. Your support is welcome, but I know I should keep away, halt any whisper of scandal and let her go to America as planned, but I'm not certain I can. I shall think on the matter further."

Chilsten stood and refilled their near-empty glasses. "Julia mentioned that Lady Miller said Miss Hall came to the estate with us. She played along, of course, but what is that about?" Chilsten asked him. "Julia wished to know."

Bellamy swore, having forgotten to tell his friends of his lie. "Her ladyship saw Miss Hall, and I could not tell her that she is now a governess. I lied and said she attended with you but was not up to house party entertainment. Thank you for not denying my words," he said, making a mental note to tell Reign of his falsehoods before too long.

Chilsten threw back his head and laughed. "Well, let us toast to Miss Hall once more being part of the upper echelons of society, just as she should be."

Bellamy raised his glass to that, hoping that mayhap such a change in status may yet be possible. "I'll toast to that." And pray he had the fortitude to deny the raging lust that thrummed through him whenever he was in Miss Hall's presence, when they were in public in any case.

TWELVE

The following day Reign stood at her bedroom window and watched as carriage after carriage left the estate. Thankfully her good friends Lord and Lady Chilsten had agreed to stay on for several more days, and she was looking forward to spending more time with her friend. Certainly, time away from the ogling eyes of the guests who had been present would be a welcome reprieve. Not to mention they would no longer need to pretend she was not a governess but a guest, since Lord Lupton-Gage could not tell the truth to Lady Miller.

Was he so ashamed of her situation in life that he could not even voice her occupation?

The situation with his lordship was not ideal, and nor did she wish for it to continue the way it was. They could not keep taunting each other whenever their paths crossed.

Not only because it was unfair to them both, but because she ought to know better. There was no future with his lordship. He had made it perfectly clear he would not marry a governess. Nor would she marry someone who would think she was good enough for him.

But that did not mean she did not crave his touch, the feel of his hands on her body, his mouth taking hers in a kiss that left her breathless and her heart racing.

She left the room and made her way to the school room, only to be handed a small written note from Mrs. Watkins that Lady Alice was with Lord and Lady Chilsten today for an outing in the carriage about Derbyshire and that her schooling would have to wait until tomorrow.

Reign refolded the note and placed it into her pocket, deciding to look at the grand gallery she had spotted during her first week here. It did not take her long to make the gallery, and she sighed at the sight of the long, wide space where family portraits had hung for hundreds of years. The large urns filled with hothouse flowers near the windows made the room smell divine.

She strolled, stopping every so often to read the names at the bottom of each painting. Some of the Lupton-Gage ancestors stared back at her with the current marquess's eyes or a twist of their lips before she came to the very man himself's portrait. He stood alone beside the mantel in his library, two wolfhounds by his feet, his daughter at his side, holding his hand and glancing lovingly up at him.

It was a charming painting and portrayed his love for Lady Alice. At least he gained a sweet daughter from his association with Lady Lupton-Gage, if nothing else before she passed.

Footsteps sounded on the wooden floors, and she glanced toward the end of the wing and found his lordship striding toward her. He was reading a missive and had not spotted her until he glanced up and skidded to a stop.

She steeled herself to be near him again and not want to throw herself at his head like some wanton. "My lord," she said, adjusting her voice to deny the emotions that were thrumming through her at the near sight of him. "Good afternoon. I hope you're having a pleasant day," she said, inwardly cringing at her question. What sort of conversation was this they were about to begin? Stale and without feeling if she were to guess. Once, they had talked for hours, sat at balls and parties, dinner events, and discussed all manner of things until he had up and married Lady Sally.

His steps slowed but continued toward her, his face schooled, so she did not know what was going through his mind. "Good afternoon, Miss Hall," he quipped, not losing stride as he passed her.

She glanced over her shoulder and watched him leave the gallery, hoping he would turn and glance at her, show her in some small way that he cared, but he did not.

Disappointment stabbed at her, and she went and sat in a window nook, looking out over the beautiful gardens and water feature the west wing overlooked.

The situation was hopeless, and maybe she ought to leave sooner than planned. She had some funds saved, and it would be enough for a passage across the Atlantic and two weeks in America for board and food. Just not as long as she had hoped to ensure security.

"Damn it, Reign," his lordship's voice barked from the end of the gallery.

Reign stood, unsure why he was back and not entirely sure she liked the savage, conflicted expression on his features. He strode purposefully toward her, clasping her face in his hands, and kissed her.

Took her lips in a searing kiss that left her reeling.

Reign clasped the lapels of his coat to steady herself, hoping her knees would not buckle at the intoxicating embrace he held her in.

His tongue tangled with hers, his hands guiding her to deepen the kiss and give him what they both wanted.

Each other.

"Bellamy," she moaned when he broke away to kiss her neck. His lips brushed beneath her ear, and she shivered, gasping. "Do not stop," she begged, wondering where her self-perseverance had disappeared to. This was not supposed to happen. They were supposed to keep away from each other.

"God, I want you," he breathed against her skin, kissing his way down to her shoulder. "I cannot keep away. God help me," he said, his voice strained, tortured.

And then he was gone. He wrenched out of her hold, leaving her reeling as he moved in the direction he had come, his back straight, his stride determined.

Reign bit her lip, his words replicating what she felt herself. She wanted him too, but there was so much between them, stopping them both.

However could they come together without everything they feared coming to fruition? Maybe they ought to jump into that abyss and find out.

BELLAMY CUPPED HIS HAND OVER HIS mouth and leaned against the wall as soon as he was out of sight of Reign. He had been so determined and doing so well when he had walked past her, ignoring her beauty and sweet gesture of welcome.

And then he had crumbled like a badly built wall with no footings or, in his case, a backbone to do as he must.

He did not stand a chance of keeping from her, stopping the scandal that would ensue unless she left his employment.

But her kisses, her longing for the same as he, he could feel it in every touch, every embrace they had.

And it was like an elixir of such he could not wean himself.

He was going to hell, that he knew without a doubt, and Reign deserved so much more than how he treated her. He could not seduce his daughter's governess. If he could not keep his hands to himself, he would have to face the scandal of marrying one's servant and fight to have her by his side, accepted as an equal in society.

The thought of her being his, to have her in his bed, sent heat to lick along his spine. They would be wild and debauched. A temptation he could not deny himself. Not if he were being honest.

There would be no stopping them once they started.

He pushed from the wall and returned to his library, pulling several parchments across his desk, determined to finish the day's work and ignore the hunger that roared through him but minutes ago.

He picked up the letter and crumpled it, throwing it into the fire, and watched as the flames turned the parchment to ash. Each time his quill touched the parchment, all he saw was Reign and what they could have if he had the strength to fight for what he wanted.

The sound of his daughter's laughter pulled him from his frustrating thoughts before the door to his library burst open, and his child ran into the room, bonnet hanging from her hand, her rosy, smiling cheeks telling him she had enjoyed her day.

"Papa, we picked mushrooms," she declared, running over to him and climbing up on his lap. "Where is Miss Hall? She will be amazed by what I found. I must tell her." She smiled as Lord and Lady Chilsten followed his daughter into the room, weary but beaming also.

"I gather the ride about Derbyshire was a success then," he said.

"Very much so." The marchioness sat on the chair opposite his desk and sighed. "And very warm. I shall seek my bed early this evening, I fear."

Chilsten ran a hand over his wife's cheek before turning to Bellamy. "How was your day, Gage? Uneventful, I hope," he asked, and Bellamy did not need to ask what he meant by such words.

He shook his head, feigning indifference, much like he had tried to do with Reign upstairs before failing miserably. "Nothing out of the ordinary, unfortunately," he lied, hoping his tone procured truth. "I have much to catch up on after the house party," he said.

"Of course," Chilsten said, watching him keenly. Something about his friend's gaze told Bellamy that Chilsten did not believe his words and was contemplating pushing the subject further.

"Miss Hall is upstairs in the gallery," he said before thinking better of it.

Chilsten raised a knowing brow, catching his eye. Bellamy averted his gaze to his daughter. "You may run along and find her and tell her of the mushrooms. I'm sure she'll be very excited for you."

"You seemed to know where Miss Hall was precisely. Are you sure your day was uneventful?" Chilsten asked after his daughter had left.

Bellamy ignored his friend's words and instead stood and rang the bell for a servant. "Tea?" he asked them, determined not to be questioned over matters he did not know how to answer.

THIRTEEN

Reign tossed and turned in her lumpy, uncomfortable bed for as long as she could stand before she had enough. She threw back the blankets and searched the end of her bed for her robe before leaving her room.

She would fetch a book to read and then try to sleep for a second time. Tonight a storm had blown in from the west, but after the hot days the Lake District had been having, the air was moist and muggy. Making sleep at the top of the house uncomfortable and all but impossible.

How she missed her cottage and the small comforts she had there, and what she wouldn't do to return to that simple life.

Pushing down the melancholy thoughts, she slipped down the main staircase, not wanting any of the servants to catch her up at this hour.

Only a few sconces burned in the foyer, but enough to see, not to mention the lightning and resulting thunder lit up the house as if a million candles were alight all at once.

She stopped at the foot of the stairs, and not hearing anyone about and not seeing any light under Lord Lupton-Gage's library door, she pushed it opened and entered.

The room was dark, and she went back into the foyer and lit her candle using a sconce before going back inside.

The scent of leather and the marquess filled her senses and made her long for things she ought not.

But after the kiss this afternoon, how could she not want to kiss him again, have his arms wrapped around her body, pulling her close, making her feel such delicious emotions?

He was addictive, and she feared that the more time she spent with him and his sweet daughter, the less appealing America became.

Not to mention she had received her first wage today from Mrs. Watkins, and the meager funds she obtained would make saving for her voyage almost triple in time.

For several minutes she studied the hundreds of books. So many to choose from in a multitude of subject matters. The choice was almost as confusing as the lord of the manor, who also tended to scramble her mind.

"Miss Hall?" a deep, masculine voice said from the door.

She started at his words, already knowing who she would find when she turned. The sight of his lordship did not disappoint. The marquess wore breeches, but no shoes, and his shirt was ruffled and not tucked into his pants. He looked as though she had pulled him from sleep, and the vision of him lying atop his bed made her warmer still.

"Lord Lupton-Gage, I could not sleep. I thought to read a book," she explained.

He entered the room, moving over to the window before wrenching it open. "The rooms have kept the heat in today, unfortunately. If you are to be in here, with a window open, it shall be much more comfortable."

She joined him at the window, the breeze going some way in cooling her down. "Mmm," she said. "How lovely that feels."

He sat on the ledge, looking out over the grounds. "I must apologize for this afternoon, Miss Hall. I should not have kissed you."

Reign did not like that he thought kissing her was a bad thing. A mistake. Well, of course it was, but there was little else to be done about it when they both desired the other.

And she was so tired of denying herself and her feelings. She could not keep being near him and remaining cold and aloof. She had never been that character, and with their shared history, it was impossible to continue.

"Bellamy," she said, tipping up his face to make him look at her. His eyes widened, but he did not try to free himself of her hold. If anything, he leaned into her touch, and that gave her the strength of conviction.

"Yes," he murmured, his voice gravelly and making her stomach clench deliciously.

She shook her head, wondering how she would say what she so desperately wanted to. "I cannot continue the way we are. To remain aloof and distant from you is impossible. You and I have a history that was stolen from us. I understand you need to put your daughter first, but I've come to a choice," she said, rallying herself to remain true to her feelings.

"And what is your choice?" he asked her, the concern, the trepidation in his blue eyes clear to see.

"I'm a woman of seven and twenty, a governess soon to set sail for America. Being here with you will be the last time I see you. I know we shall never cross paths after my time here comes to an end, and I do not want a few stolen kisses to be all that is between us," she admitted, praying he did not think less of her for being so candid.

He pulled her down to sit on the windowsill with him. "What do you want, Reign?" he asked, holding her hands, his fingers intertwining with hers.

"I want you," she admitted, voicing what she

had so long denied herself, and he too, she supposed. "For as long as I'm here I want to be with you." She glanced down at their entwined fingers. "I know that I'm taking a risk, and I was hoping that you may know some ways to reduce that risk since you're more worldly than I, but I want to be with you. For as long as we can, in secret, a sweet sin that only you and I know of. My friend Lady Chilsten would guide me against doing such a thing, but I—"

His lips took hers, halting her words, and she reached for him, pulled him close, and let desire sweep her away. He was everything she had always wanted. The man she had once hoped to marry.

While life had not played fair and she had lost him to a scandalous woman, she could only assume by his kiss that he felt the same as she.

"Yes," he breathed against her lips. "For as long as we have, I want you too. But are you sure, really sure, Reign? This is a risk, and it is a lot to ask of you."

She shrugged, having long ago given up hope for such a sweet end, a completion that would conclude with her as his wife. Life was not always fair, but that did not mean one could not make the best of a bad situation.

"I'm sure. I've never been more sure of anything in my life."

* * *

DENY HER. STOP THIS MADNESS.

The words slammed about in his mind, but he could not heed them. For so many years, he had lived without the one woman who had made him burn, and now, here she was, offering herself to him for as long as she stayed in Derbyshire, and he could not refuse her.

Devil take him, he could not say no.

He kissed her again, taking her lips. She kissed him back, eager for his touch, willing to feel him in ways she had never done before.

His body burned, his cock stood to attention, and he knew there was no turning back. Not now. Now, he had a glimpse of what the next few weeks or months could mean for them both—days of stolen kisses and nights of wicked touches—endless bliss and comfort in each other's arms.

Damn it all to hell. He wanted her so bad it physically hurt. And now, all he had ever wished for was within reach.

"Reign," he moaned, her tongue driving him to distraction. She pushed against him, her breasts free from restraints, her shift and robe barely enough to keep her modest.

Not that he intended to keep her modest for long. He would have her, make love to her, give her what they both wanted and pray that when judgment day came, God would forgive him.

"Tell me what you want. I will give you anything you ask for. You merely have to say it," he said.

She pulled from him, her eyes shimmering with unshed tears, her lips swollen from his kisses. She had never looked more beautiful and disheveled than she was.

"I want you to make love to me. I want to go with you to your room." She bit her lip, her eyes filled with trepidation.

He stood and pulled her to stand before leading her from the library. Thankfully the house remained quiet, the servants long to bed as he led her up the staircase toward his chambers.

He stopped at his door, turning the handle and swinging it open. Without a word, he scooped her up in his arms, kissing her quickly. "We should have had this, you and I. But tonight, and the days ahead, you are mine, and I am yours. Do you agree?"

She nodded, and without further ado, he crossed the threshold of his bedchamber, kicking the door closed with his foot—and the door on the judgemental, unfair world around them—wrapping them together in a place meant just for them.

FOURTEEN

Reign shivered as Bellamy slid her down his hard, delicious body she had admired for so long that she could no longer remember when she had first noticed him.

London, of course, during her coming out. But now, she was allowed to touch and be with him as she had always dreamed. She was possibly going to Hades for her actions.

Even with his aversion to scandal and his honesty about trying to keep his daughter free from it ought to keep her away, but she could not. She would do all she could to keep their love affair from being known, but she would no longer stay away.

Her heart thumped hard in her chest as he stepped back, wrenching his shirt over his head. His stomach was all hard and chiseled planes, and without thought, she reached out and ran her hand over his form.

His eyes burned with need, and she shivered, biting her lip. His stomach rose and fell with each breath, and she could almost taste his desire in the air.

"I have always wondered what you looked like under your superfine suits. How well you do," she admitted, grinning.

His chuckle was gravelly and low. "Then that makes two of us, my darling, for I have always wondered what you look like, too, under your pretty gowns," he said, reaching for the little ribbons on her stays that protected her modesty. He untied them, a small grin playing about his lips before he pushed her robe from her shoulders.

It pooled at her feet, and she stepped out of it, wanting to be free from any restraints.

His eyes met hers, and she read the question in his. "Would you like to do the honors?" she teased, raising one questioning brow.

He nodded, his swallow almost audible. "Hell, yes, I would," he answered, reaching for her shift and slipping it from her body with more care than she expected.

She stood before him, naked, but no fear thrummed through her veins. Oh no. Not when Bellamy watched her with such adoration and hunger that she could be nothing but secure in his presence.

Reign stepped against him, his hard muscles, his jutting manhood pressing against her stomach. She undulated against him, wanting to feel more of him, wanting her body to feel this pleasure even without being as intimate as they soon would be.

"You feel so damn good," he said, scooping her up into his arms a second time and striding over to the bed.

They tumbled onto the soft, opulent bedding, and Reign opened for him, wrapping her legs about his waist. He teased her sex, undulating against her mons and sending a delightful thrum through her body.

Expectation was heavy in the air as he lay atop her. The hair on his chest tickled her, and she kissed him deep and long. She had wanted him for such a long time, had been so sure she had lost him forever, but now was her chance.

He kissed her back, and their tongues tangled, played, and teased.

"This may hurt a little," he warned her.

She nodded, ready to become a woman, to be with him wholly. She did not have to wait long. He thrust into her, joined with her completely, and she gasped.

He kissed her, murmuring sweet words of comfort as the pain ebbed away.

"I'm sorry," he said. "Are you well, my darling?"

She nodded, wiggling a little to adjust to his size. The feeling was odd and different, but not terrible. If anything, she felt a warm awakening within her soul, one she wanted more of.

"I'm fine," she said, holding him close. "Do not stop."

He did not. He thrust into her with care at first before his pace increased. With every stroke, Reign could feel her body calling out, seeking something out of reach.

"You feel so damn good, my darling. How I have dreamed of this moment, God save my soul," he said, kissing her deep and long.

"Me too," she divulged before he took her lips again, and she was lost. Lost in the arms of the one man she had always adored.

Whom she had always loved.

Bellamy.

BELLAMY FOUGHT TO CONTROL HIS emotions. Guilt and desire plagued him in equal parts. He ought not to be here, sleeping with Reign, but nor could he deny her anything.

Or himself, when it came down to it.

Marry her and bedamn the ton and what they think. Do not use her in this way, and not offer your hand.

She pulled him closer still, and for a moment, he forgot the warning words in his mind. She was so hot and tight, the one woman he had longed and desired from the first moment he had seen her in London.

And now she was here. In his arms and giving herself to him willingly. No headier elixir was there in life.

How he wished he could go back, change both their pasts.

He took her, claimed her as should have always been his right, and she welcomed him, opened for him like a flower ready for picking.

"Bellamy," she gasped as the first tremors rocked her body.

He fought not to spend as she came apart in his arms, enjoying her pleasure as it ricocheted through her. "Enjoy me," he told her before her body, pulling against his cock, dragged his release forward.

He shouted her name and withdrew, spilling his seed over the sheets. He could not risk her becoming pregnant. He had already ruined her life many years ago. He would be careful not to do so again.

Except you could ruin her just by being intimate with Reign, even if a child is not conceived ...

He ignored his thoughts and slumped beside her, pulling her into the crook of his arm. She came willingly, slipping one leg over his, her hand settled on his chest, playing with his body.

Her touch sent fire to course through his veins, and he wondered if it would always be like this between them. A wildness that was untamed, uninhabited, and improper.

"Bellamy," she sighed, snuggling into his side. "How wonderful you are. I had always wondered what it would be like to be with a man just so, but you have exceeded all my expectations," she teased him.

He grinned down at her, kissing her forehead quickly. "I hope when you wondered about the sexual act that you only ever thought about it with me and no one else." He shifted so he could see her eyes clearer. "I think I shall be very jealous indeed if I find out you ever lusted over anyone else."

She grinned, kissing his chest before biting it playfully. His cock jumped, and he groaned. "No, you are the only man I ever wanted where you are right at this moment. Can I hope that I am the same for you?"

He nodded, rubbing her back with his hand. "You know I was tricked in London, and the missive Sally had delivered to me was addressed from you," he admitted to her, having never told anyone of the deceiving nature of his wife that night. "I thought it would be you I would meet in that conservatory."

Reign sat up, staring at him, her eyes wide with shock. "No, that cannot be true. Lady Lupton-Gage would not be so cruel to steal you away in such a way and break my heart. I know I did not know her so very well, but surely a lady of her breeding could not be so horrible. I always believed the note was from her, and you foolishly did as she asked."

One of the reasons why Bellamy had fallen for Reign hard and quick in London. She had been truthful, honest, and brutally beautiful. In his opinion, she should have been the Season's diamond.

She was certainly his jewel.

"Sally was not a nice woman or anything like the perfect debutante she made herself out to be. She only married me for my money and status. She never wanted me in any way and made that clear after our wedding night." He shivered at the memory of that evening and how cold and disinterested she had been. He had felt as though he were forcing her, and he had not touched her again. Not that she cared, not when she admitted to wanting to travel without him or their child.

"Oh, Bellamy," Reign said, reaching out to touch her palm to his cheek. He leaned into her touch, having been denied a woman's comfort for too many years. "I'm so sorry that this happened to you. To us both. I can understand why you do not mourn Lady Lupton-Gage as a husband might as much as it shames me to say so."

He nodded, but guilt savaged his soul at her belief in him. He was not a fine example of gentlemanly behavior by criticizing his wife. Not to mention he ought to make what they had done right and offer to marry Reign. Not appear to use her to slake his own lust while she lived under his roof as a governess.

He ought to be horsewhipped for being so brazen, but instead, he kissed her and lost himself and his conscience in her arms.

FIFTEEN

Reign found the mathematical lessons with Lady Alice difficult to keep forthright in her mind the following morning. Her introspections kept drifting back to the evening before and what she and Bellamy had shared.

She shivered at the memory of his touch. Her body already craving more of what he had gifted her.

She had woken almost before dawn and crept upstairs to her room without being seen. She awoke at daybreak, her body feeling lethargic and the most relaxed it had ever felt in her life.

She grinned, knowing the reason why. Not to mention she could not wait to have Bellamy alone once more. Already she missed his handsome face and interesting conversation.

"Miss Hall," Lady Alice said, glancing up at her with her sweet little face. She had her chalkboard before her, doing some number writing, and Reign could see she was also thinking about something else.

"Yes?" she answered, curious to hear what the little girl wanted to know. She was an intelligent child and observant.

"Why are you not married? My parents were married, and Lord and Lady Chilsten are married, but you are not," she said, a little frown between her brow as if this information troubled her.

Reign smiled, having wondered at that question a time or two. Yet she had always had the same answer—because she was tricked out of her love and lost everything after that fact.

"I suppose because I've not been asked, and I'm not in love. I think a lady ought to love her husband and have those feelings returned to make a good match, and I've not found that," she said in half-truths.

While she had never been asked, she had once been on the cusp of a proposal.

"I hope that you are married one day. Mrs. Watkins says that governesses are pariahs who live on the outskirts of society and are not accepted belowstairs either. Are you happy, Miss Hall?" the little girl asked her, her frown deepening.

Reign schooled her features, wondering what Mrs. Watkins meant when saying such things to a child. "I'm happy, and I'm delighted to be teaching you, which is enough," she said, unsure why the housekeeper would say something so troubling to a five-year-old. While she knew that she was not accepted above stairs or below due to her station, she had hoped she was gaining friendships with the servants, but perhaps that was all in her mind.

"My mama has passed away, but Mrs. Watkins says no one is ever really gone. Do you believe that, Miss Hall?" she asked.

Reign frowned, wondering if Bellamy had explained how life and death worked. From the little girl's words, it seemed he had not, and she certainly would not be the one to do so.

"I'm certain when you're an old lady with a wonderful life behind you, that you will see your mama again," Reign said, wishing it would be the case for the child's sake if nothing else.

"Papa misses Mama, and I miss her too," she said, picking up her piece of chalk once more. "You will have to leave when Mama returns. Mrs. Watkins said that Mama does not like pretty ladies, and you're so pretty Miss Hall, that Mama will surely be jealous."

Reign could not form the words to reply to such a statement, nor would she allow Mrs. Watkins to continue speaking to the little girl in such a way. What happened between his lordship and his wife in the past was not something the housekeeper ought to be speaking of in any manner at all, least of all to his lordship's daughter.

"Now, let us look at letters next," Reign said, turning to her chalkboard as she wrote down the alphabet. "Can you write these down for me?" she asked Lady Alice and took a relieved breath when the little girl dropped the odd conversation.

"Ah, here you both are," Lord Lupton-Gage said from the doorway, smiling at his daughter as she yelped at the sight of him before running in his direction and hugging his legs.

Bellamy winked and grinned at Reign, and pleasure flooded her. She wished she, too, could run up to him and hold him as his daughter was free to do.

"What are we learning this morning?" he asked, picking up his daughter, who started to list off all the lessons they had learned so far. Reign packed up the school room, readying the space for the little girl's lunch.

"I know Mrs. Watkins has your lunch in the nursery today if you've finished your lessons?" he asked, glancing at Reign.

She nodded. "We have, for now."

The little girl wiggled to get down and, without another word, ran down the hall toward the nursery.

His lordship stood in the doorway, watching her, his eyes heavy with determination, and she shivered, wondering what was going on in that handsome head of his.

He glanced out into the passageway and then entered the room, closing the door behind him.

The moment the door clicked shut, Reign dashed into his arms. Their mouths clashed, his hands everywhere. Her body burned with a need that surpassed all logical thought. They were in the school room. Anyone, staff and Lord and Lady Chilsten alike, could come across them at any moment, but she did not care.

She wanted his hands on her, to touch her, to make her feel alive after so long of feeling nothing at all.

For years she had led the life of the spinster Miss Hall who had suffered a failed Season. The town of Grafton knew it, and no doubt London as well.

To be here now, in Bellamy's arms, was a gift she could not refuse, as much as she should.

His hands slipped about her waist, and he turned her, pressing her against the door. His manhood pressed against her through her gown, and warmth pooled at her core.

"I want you so much, Reign," he murmured against her lips, watching her as he pressed harder against her sex. A delicious sensation thrummed through her, and she clutched at his shoulders, wanting him too.

"Yes," she breathed. "When can we be alone again?" she asked.

He kissed her, deep and long, his hungry mouth taking hers in a way that left her breathless, if not witless. "Tonight. I shall dismiss Chambers early and ensure the staff does not loiter upstairs. Come to my room," he said, kissing her nose and gifting her with a mischievous grin before he stepped back.

The moment he parted from her, she missed his heat, his very presence. She wanted to reach out and pull him to her again, but did not. "I will," she said.

Reign stepped out of the way, moving back to where the chalkboards were as his lordship opened the door. The moment he did, Mrs. Watkins was standing on the other side, her eyes wide at the sight of them standing in the room.

Alone ...

Reign schooled her features, not wanting the housekeeper to hate her any more than she already did, and nor did she need her to think something was between her and Lord Lupton-Gage. Her working life would be harder again if she did.

"Mrs. Watkins," his lordship stated, moving out into the passage. "Were you looking for me? Miss Hall and I have just been discussing Alice's learning." He crossed his arms over his chest and looked down on the older woman, whose displeased visage was clear to read to both of them.

"Lady Alice would like you to join her, my lord. I said I would come and ask." She threw a displeased glare in Reign's direction.

"Very well, I shall go directly," he said, glancing back at Reign. "Good afternoon, Miss Hall."

Reign dipped into a curtsy. "Good day, my lord," she said before his clipped footsteps echoed down the hall.

No sooner was he gone did Mrs. Watkins round on her. "I do not know what game you're playing, Miss Hall, but this one is not for you. His lordship cannot marry you and would not even if he could. You must, for your own reputation, stop whatever madness I came across today."

For several moments Reign could not speak. Never had she been confronted so pointedly before in her life. And while she admired the older woman for her gumption, she was already too late for the warning.

She knew the risks she took and that his lordship would not marry her to protect his daughter from any more scandal. And while such truths hurt, they were not enough to scare her away from clutching the smallest amount of happiness she could while she was here.

"As his lordship stated, we were merely discussing Lady Alice's schooling. I do not appreciate your accusation, Mrs. Watkins. I thought better of you," she said, hoping her cool response would take the older woman off guard.

It did not.

"You are a foolish woman, which I did not think you were at our first meeting, but I see I am wrong. You will pay a heavy price for this folly that will not end as you wish. Do not say I did not warn you, Miss Hall. And do not come crying to me when you need help," she said, turning on her heel and leaving Reign alone.

Reign sighed, slumping down on the small child-size chair. She was being foolish and possibly would regret her actions, but nor could she stop this madness. Bellamy was an elixir that she could not wean herself from. And right at this moment, she did not want to, no matter what Mrs. Watkins or anyone thought.

Sixteen

Bellamy paced the library the following morning after Reign did not come to his bedroom the night before. He sent a note requesting her presence after Alice's schooling was complete for the day, and then he would find out the reason why.

Not that he did not already have a good idea why it was that she did not come to him.

His housekeeper appeared to have been listening at the schoolroom door yesterday, and if that were the case, then she would have heard their conversation behind those few inches of wood.

Not that she would talk, she would lose her job if her lips started to tattle about the house, but it did not mean that she had not warned Reign away.

Which, much to his annoyance, seemed to have been the case and worked.

A light knock sounded on his door. "Enter," he barked, taking a calming breath when Reign entered the room, her eyes wide at his tone.

"Come in, Miss Hall," he said, his tone gentler. "Have a seat here." He gestured to the chair sitting across from his desk before he sat, trying to pick his words carefully and in a tone that was not as annoyed as he felt.

Not that he had any right to be annoyed. Reign did not owe him anything, not even loyalty, if she chose otherwise. He had told her that he would not marry her. Scandal his excuse and that was the truth. But he could throw all that others thought and would say about his marriage to her and do what he wanted.

Marry her.

He was a bastard even to enter any kind of liaison with Reign and offer her nothing. She deserved so much better than he was giving her.

She sat, clasping her hands in her lap. She appeared uncomfortable, and he hated placing her in this position.

"You did not come to me last evening. Is something troubling you?" he asked, knowing that there was and certain he knew the reason why.

She glanced down at her hands, wringing them, and it took all his patience not to demand to know what had happened the moment he left the schoolroom yesterday afternoon.

"I think Mrs. Watkins suspects us, and she has warned me away from you. Stated that if it were marriage I was after that I would not get it," she said, meeting his eyes but once during her explanation.

He ran a hand through his hair. He ought to confront his housekeeper and tell her to mind her own goddamn business, but his housekeeper was right in warning Reign away. And he was wrong to try to seduce her back to his side.

"You have been honest with me," she continued. "I understand why we can never marry." She paused, biting her lip and glancing out onto the garden from his library windows. "I adore Lady Alice and would not wish to hurt her either by the scandal that would break in London should they hear of our union. Of you marrying your daughter's governess after your wife was less than discreet abroad, but it is still a reminder that you are what I will never have. As much as we may come together in secret, you will never own me in public. I think Mrs. Watkins reminded me of that fact more than anything else."

While his housekeeper knew a great deal about his country estate here in Derbyshire, she did not know all the truth. She did not know that he cared for Reign beyond reason. She was everything to him and having her here at his estate, the truth of his feelings had only doubled.

Marry her ...

"I know I am being a bastard. I should not touch one hair on your innocent head, and yet, I cannot stay away. Just as I could not stay away when we were in London together."

She met his eyes, and the pain and disappointment he read in her blue gaze tore him in two. He did not want her to be upset, to be torn over what was right and wrong, what she ought to do versus what was expected of her.

"I know," she sighed. "I feel the same way about you. While Mrs. Watkins did warn me, the entire time I kept thinking that I did not care. Not really. I only stayed away last evening because Miss Rivers, the scullery maid on my floor, slept with her door open, and I had to pass her room to reach the stairs. I think Mrs. Watkins put her up to it and requested that she keep an eye on me all night."

Bellamy ground his teeth at the infuriating, meddlesome housekeeper he employed. She ought to know her place and ignore what he did with his staff.

The thought shamed him.

To think such a way was unfair and not something he would approve of. Mrs. Watkins was in her position for a reason, and the welfare of her staff was paramount.

"I ought to move you back onto the first floor," he said.

Reign jumped to her feet, coming about the desk to stand before him. "No, you must not. That will make me look even more the besotted fool than I already do to everyone belowstairs."

"Mrs. Watkins is not everyone," he said, reaching out to take her hand and link his fingers with hers.

"You know what I mean." She gave a small smile of resignation. "I'm not much liked as it is, and your butler disapproves of my presence. I'm certain he thinks bad of me," she said, shaking her head. "No, I must stay where I am to lower suspicion," she informed him.

"I will speak to them both and ensure you are not harassed. And if you would like, I shall keep away from you. Keep our association one that is platonic and professional only." The words tasted like vinegar on his tongue, yet they had to be said. He did not want Reign to feel uncomfortable under his roof, nor did he want her to think he only wanted her for one thing.

He did not.

If he had the choice, if he could alter time, he would change all of his past. Have Reign be the woman he was caught with in London. Marry her, have children with her.

She would make a wonderful mother, just as she was a tremendous governess.

She stepped closer to him, and he had to lean

back in his chair to look up at her. "I do not want to be scared away from you by some housekeeper. I like what we have, what we're doing together," she said, a wicked grin on her lips. "I lost what I wanted due to another's selfish deeds many years ago. I shall not be bullied away from taking what little happiness I can have now for as long as I'm here. I'm sick of people determining my life and telling me what I can and cannot do. I shall do what I want, and that is my choice."

He stared at her, unable to believe, to hope, she was in earnest.

ANGER THRUMMED THROUGH HER AT THE thought of Bellamy being torn away from her yet again. If they were careful no scandal would break and she could be with him for as long as she remained here.

Which, if her pitiful wage was any indication, may be longer than she expected.

But no matter, she did not mind living in the lovely Lake District, and nor did she mind having Bellamy in her bed.

"Do you really mean that?" he asked her, reaching for her and pulling her onto his lap.

She nodded, slipping her arms around his neck and playing with the hair at his nape. "I do mean it. Every word. I know what I agreed to and what price I was willing to pay to be with you.

We are breaking no vows. That is enough for me," she said, leaning forward and kissing him quickly.

He clasped the back of her head and held her close, deepening the kiss.

Heat pooled at her core, and she wiggled, needing to be closer. His touch slipped down her leg, and he seized a good portion of her gown, dragging it over her thigh. Cool air kissed her skin, and expectation thrummed in her veins.

What wickedness did he have up his sleeve now?

She met his eye, seeing mischief burning in his blue gaze.

"What are you doing?" she asked, sucking in a startled breath when his hand brushed across her sex.

"Oh, my darling. You weep for me here," he said, teasing her further.

She moaned. Would it always be like this with him? Would she always crave his touch, his kisses?

"Tell me what you're going to do," she begged him, like a wanton.

"You will see," he teased, pushing her legs farther apart.

Reign stilled, her body on a precipice of expectation before his hand slid over her mons and across her sex, pressing upward in a teasing stroke.

She moaned again, lifting herself toward his touch. "Yes," she breathed. "I wanted this. I need this from you."

He dipped his fingers into her sex, watching her as he took her with his hand. Played and teased her sex with exquisite ability. Reign bit her lip as his touch taunted her toward release.

Now that she knew what pleasure could be had, she could not get enough of Bellamy. Nor would she deny him anything.

She wanted him as much as he wanted her.

"Do not stop," she pleaded, kissing him. Their tongues tangled, their breathing one. He was all maddening sweet rogue, the man she had always adored and now who held so much more than mere affection in her heart.

She did not want to name the emotions coiling within her, but even so, they were there, simmering, longing, wanting to come out.

"You drive me to distraction," he said, his eyes wild with determination.

Reign pushed against him, seeking him deeper, harder, faster. Pleasure burst from within her, thrumming through her body. "Bellamy," she gasped, holding him, hoping she did not scream too loudly for anyone to hear.

"Enjoy me, my darling," he said, the endearment making her heart beat faster. The satisfaction of hearing the words almost more pleasurable than the act itself. She rode his hand, not caring how she appeared or if they were come upon. Her center focused on the man in her arms and no one else.

And she doubted she would ever focus on anyone else again.

SEVENTEEN

The following morning Bellamy sat at his desk, reviewing the ledgers his steward had left for him to consider, when a letter marked for Miss Hall caught his attention on the silver salver.

He picked it up and read the inscription, noting it was marked from Grafton. Did it have something to do with the sale of her cottage?

He rang the bell, summoning a footman who entered post haste.

"My lord," the young man said from the doorway.

"Fetch Miss Hall and bring her to the library. She has correspondence," he said, wanting to explain just in case his housekeeper had been partaking in loose lips downstairs.

The young man nodded, hastily going to make his request, and it was only a short time later that Reign knocked and entered.

He gestured for her to sit across from him.

Her timid smile made his heart beat fast, and he was thankful for the few feet of mahogany that separated them. He could not keep away from her at the best of times, and it was no different even now when they had business to discuss.

They had come together just yesterday in this very room, and he could not take such a risk again, certainly not when the door remained unlocked and partially open.

"My lord?" she queried. "Is all well?"

He nodded, wanting to put her at rest. "There is nothing wrong between us," he whispered, smiling at her. "But there is news from Grafton. A letter has arrived for you, and I thought you might wish to read it to see what it's concerning." He slid the letter over to her.

Her eyes widened at the news, and she glanced at the letter before leaning forward and picking it up. "It looks to be from Mr. Turnball, the local magistrate who's looking after the sale of my cottage. He was a good friend of Papa and had been helping me with my finances, or lack thereof, before I came here," she explained, breaking the seal.

He watched her read the missive, a frown marring her brow. She glanced over at him before staring back down at the letter. "Is everything well, Reign?" he asked, growing concerned at her silence.

"I do not understand," she said at length, studying the parchment. "I do not know a Mr. Gerald Hall from Brighton. I'm certain they have the wrong relative," she said, placing the missive back on the desk.

"Wrong message to whom and what about?" he asked her again.

She met his eyes, flicking the letter across the desk to him. He scanned it quickly, surprised by what he was reading. "It says your cottage has sold, and a distant relative has left you and two cousins of yours, several times removed, funds from his estate." He met her eyes, seeing that she still held doubts. "It says you have inherited one hundred pounds. This is good news, Reign," he said, hoping she would be happy. "You have enough funds to leave for America if that is still what you wish. Or," he suggested, fighting to keep the grin from his lips. "You could return to London with Lady Chilsten, a woman of some independence, to have another Season."

"But why would I have another Season?" she argued. "I do not want anyone to court me. I'm quite happy with who has seized my eye here," she teased, mischief in her gaze. She bit her lip, reading the missive again. "While it is a good sum of money and enough to keep me for some time, there is much to consider."

"And you do not need to decide straight-away," he added, perhaps more eager than he should be. He certainly did not want her to leave for America, but then what? Did he wish her to stay? Become his mistress?

The thought shamed him. He could not do that to her either. Not after all she had been through and lost. "The letter states the names of Miss Evie Hall and Miss Arabella Hall. Do you know either lady?" he asked her, having never heard of them himself. It was doubtful that either woman had Seasons in London or was part of society. "Maybe you would like to meet them before you decide to leave England or not?"

"I do not know them, but I would like to, but it doesn't say much about them in the letter, only that they were both in service in the south of England." She sighed. "Perhaps they were born to country gentlemen like myself but also fell on hard times." She shrugged. "Either way, it seems they had to go away to work. It is a shame that women always bear the brunt of men's mistakes, whether those mistakes be financial or emotional."

Bellamy met her eyes and saw the moment she comprehended her own words and how they related to him. A fair point and one he would not disabuse her of.

"I have certainly made bad choices in the past, but I'm trying to make amends for them, so my daughter does not suffer the same decision you had to make. Maybe not concerning wealth, but certainly in standing. I wish it had been different for you, Reign. When I think about how much you have struggled these past years, the very thought repulses me."

REIGN NODDED, WISHING HE DID NOT care so much about what other people thought or what society expected of men and women. If he did not, there could have been a chance that he would have offered marriage to her after the year of mourning his wife, but he had not.

So traumatized or angered by his wife's conduct meant that everyone else, even herself, had to pay for Lady Lupton-Gage's sins.

He would not marry her, certainly not now she was a governess. Even if she did return to London with Lady Chilsten, that did not mean people would believe what had been said of her while at the house party. For years she worked as a governess in Grafton, certainly that had never been a secret.

She ought to take her small inheritance, visit her cousins she never knew she had, and leave England. Make a fresh start. Marry a man who did not care what life had thrown at them and live to the fullest.

She leaned back against the chair, staring out the windows, debating doing just that.

"I'm a selfish man. I know I am, but I do not want you to go. I want to keep you here forever."

"Then marry me," she asked of him, no longer willing to ignore their affliction. "Marry me, and I will be able to stay. If not, you know I must go, whether to America or London. Maybe not today or next week, but I shall have to leave you sometime."

The words hurt to speak, but they were the truth. His fear of marrying down, of causing more scandal for his name and daughter, guided all his thoughts and actions, except with her. She was his Achilles heel, his past, once maybe the woman who held his heart and had never relinquished it. She was the reason he had settled into this secret love affair because when it came to her, he could not say no.

He rocked back in his chair, watching her and the hairs on her skin lifted at his savage, hungry regard. She swallowed, on edge all of a sudden, as if she were in a dangerous situation that she did not know how to escape.

She raised her chin, meeting his stare head-on. "Is that not the case, my lord?" she asked, demanding clarification.

He pushed up from his seat and came toward her. She reminded herself that he would not hurt her, even if her words may have bestowed truths he did not want to hear. Did not want to face.

He pulled her up from her chair and wrenched her into his hold. "You know I would have married you had not the late marchioness ensured I did not. I wanted you as my wife, my lover, everything, but now it is all different. It is not only us we have to think of. I know this hurts you. It rips me in two," he said, laying his forehead against hers, his hold unbreakable. "I wish you never came here as a governess. I cannot further add to my family's scandalous name by marrying you."

Reign clasped his face, making him look at her. "What we're doing is unfair to both of us, but mostly to me. I take the risk, and my reputation will not be saved should I get with a child. A choice I made to be with you, I know, but it is madness, Bellamy. I cannot be your whore forever. Surely that is not what you want for me. I have too much respect for myself to continue in this way forever. Marrying me would lessen the scandal should it be discovered that I'm bedding you, and are your daughter's governess."

A muscle worked in his jaw as he thought over her words. "I understand." He sighed, pulling back to look at her. His hands dropped from her waist, and he kneeled instead.

Reign stared at him. Her body shook as he met her eyes and reached for her hand. "You are right, Miss Hall. I cannot, as a gentleman, continue to let you live in such sin. I would be no better than a cad. I will not allow that for you or me, so will you marry me instead? I am the gentleman, after all. It should be I who proposes," he quipped.

EIGHTEEN

Reign stared at him, dumbfounded for several moments. "Are you truly in earnest? Are you willing to dismiss any rumors of my being here? Defend my honor," she teased, grinning.

Bellamy nodded, having never meant anything more in his life. But he could not lose Reign again, scandal or no scandal. He could not watch her be devastated all over again by his decision.

"There are ways to limit any scandal that may ensue. My lie of you being a guest here at the house party is fortunate."

She frowned and pulled him to stand. "You lied about me? When?" she asked him.

He wrapped his arms around her waist, enjoying the fact more and more that he could already touch her as he liked. "I was questioned about you when a guest saw you in the gardens. I fumbled and stated you had arrived with Lady Chilsten but did not feel up to attending the parlor games and outings."

Reign started to giggle and then laugh, and he rolled his eyes. "I know, hearing the excuse sounds absurd now, but I panicked, and it was the first thing that popped into my head," he explained.

"I'm not ashamed of being a governess, Bellamy. There are worse professions I could have procured."

He squeezed her tighter, not wanting to imagine such a tragedy. "Do not say such things. I cannot bare it." He paused. "Lord and Lady Chilsten are still here, and Lady Chilsten is the sister to many influential families in England. With some assistance, the notion that you were ever employed here can be squashed and forgotten about soon enough. We will say you arrived, we courted as we once had in London, and we're to marry."

Her happiness all but glowed from her skin, and he sighed a relieved breath, knowing she was his again.

His heart.

His love.

Love?

The word bounced about in his mind, and yet it did not scare him. If anything, it motivated him and enlightened him to push to have her redeemed. To be returned to the center of society and the place which should have always been hers.

"For a gentleman who only thought to propose, you seem to have everything in hand and sorted." Her smile lit up the room, and her eyes filled with tears. "You are in earnest, Bellamy, aren't you? You truly wish to marry me?" she asked him again.

He nodded, the overwhelming joy he felt within telling him this had been the correct course all along. "Say yes, Reign, so that I can kiss you," he teased, feeling far more joyous and alive than he had in years.

They were always meant to be together. They had always meant to be married. Had Sally and her underhanded ways not torn them from each other, they would have been married years ago.

But nothing stood in their way now.

"Yes," she answered him. "Yes, I shall marry you."

He wrenched her into his arms, taking her lips in a kiss that would forever remain in his mind. She kissed him back, and he could feel the dampness of her tears on his cheeks.

His heart burst with what he felt for the woman in his arms. He had wronged her multiple times, but no longer. From today onward, he would own his mistakes and the errors of his past and move forward. Fight for what he wanted.

Fight for her ...

"Oh, do excuse me," Lord Chilsten said from the doorway.

Bellamy reluctantly let Reign go, and she turned toward their unwanted guests, her cheeks high with color.

"Lord and Lady Chilsten," she mumbled, her eyes wide with alarm. "We were ... we were just discussing ..."

"Our forthcoming marriage," Bellamy blurted, taking Reign's hand in his. "And I shall need your assistance in London to ensure the scandal of my marrying my daughter's governess is not overshadowed by how I feel about the woman to be my marchioness," he said.

Lady Chilsten clapped her hands and ran toward Reign, hugging her fiercely, both ladies laughing and talking simultaneously so that even Bellamy could not understand what they were uttering.

Lord Chilsten came over to him, smiling. "Congratulations, my friend. I am glad you have seen sense and have made a choice that will be good for you and your daughter." He walked over to the decanter of brandy, pouring four glasses and handing Bellamy one. "What is this plan of yours?" he asked before going back to hand Lady Chilsten and Reign a glass too.

"Well, as to that," he said, explaining what he had told Reign earlier of how she was never here as a governess but a guest who came to visit with Lady Chilsten and not so much take part in the house party.

"It is a sound idea and coincides with your fibbing, Lord Lupton-Gage," Julia chided. "I think we can make it work, so long as Reign returns to London with us, with you following to have the banns called in Town. A unified assault against any impending chatter is what we need to do, but I think it's winnable. So long as your staff says nothing about Miss Hall working here these past weeks."

"I shall deal with the servants and ensure no one mentions her being here before the house party. But my staff have never given me cause for concern before. I'm certain they shall not want to when they hear my decision," he said, meeting Reign's gaze and seeing the uncertainty in hers.

"Mrs. Watkins does not like me, Bellamy. I'm not so sure she will be amenable to your proposal of me becoming her mistress. She warned me away from you only days ago, remember?"

Bellamy ground his teeth, not appreciating Mrs. Watkins interfering in his life and choices. He would address the situation with her first before they left for London.

"I will discuss the matter with them all, but now, let us share a toast to our betrothal." Bellamy pulled Reign beside him, holding her close. He did not like it when she was so far away, and the thought of her living with Lord and Lady Chilsten in London, no longer under his roof, made the calling of the banns more urgent than he first thought.

"To us," he said, raising his glass. "To our marriage and future happiness."

The others cheered, sipping from the glasses. "To you both. We wish you both very happy," Lady Chilsten stated. "And now to London, where we can move forward with this special day sooner rather than later," she quipped.

Reign laughed, and Bellamy dipped his head, stealing a kiss from his future wife. "I could not agree more."

THEY SET OFF FOR LONDON TWO DAYS later, and Reign watched as Bellamy adjusted himself in his seat across from her. He had requested and been granted her company in the carriage until they reached their first inn for the night.

"You know you should not have demanded Lord and Lady Chilsten to allow me to travel with you without a maid. It's highly scandalous, and we all know how much you dislike scandal," she teased him.

He grinned back at her, and she shook her head at his gumption. The man was impossible to say no to. It seemed not even their friends were able to deny him any request.

"I wanted you with me, and we're so far north that no disgrace will ensue, nothing that will be seen in any case," he said, wiggling his brows. "We will arrive in London, announce our engagement, squash any talk of you being a governess, and all will be well."

She raised her brow, not so certain that everyone in London would believe their tale. Not when guests at house parties talked to servants, and Reign was not so green that she did not think Lady Miller had asked that question while in attendance.

She reached out and took his hand. "Even if there is a scandal, Bellamy, it will not last forever. Certainly, it will not last thirteen years until Alice has her coming out. There will be far more interesting things for the *ton* to sink their teeth into by then. Please do not worry too much," she said, hoping he would listen and forget about his late wife and all the strife she caused. None of it was his fault, and he ought not to carry the burden around with him.

"Are you saying, Miss Hall, that you think I worry too much?" He rubbed a hand over his stomach, cringing. "My doctor does suggest I stop troubling myself, but it is a hard habit to break. I've been doing it for so long now."

Too long, in Reign's opinion. She hoped, in time, she could rid Bellamy of any thoughts or memories of his late wife. She had not been worthy of the title in the first place.

Reign slipped over to sit beside him. His eyes darkened in expectation and the air thickened with need. "Would you like me to distract you, my lord?" she asked in a sultry tone, running her hand over his suit jacket.

He raised his brow, wonder in his eyes. "What did you have in mind?" he asked.

She slid her hand down his abdomen, enjoying the feel of his muscular form beneath her palm before touching his thigh. But she did not stop there. Instead, she touched the growing bulge in his pants, stroking it as he liked.

He covered her hand with his, pressing harder against his manhood. "You undo me, Reign," he said, his gaze dipping to her lips in a manner that made heat pool at her core.

Without thought, she slid to her knees and kneeled before him. She reached for his falls, unbuttoning his pants, wanting to see him, view what gave her so much pleasure.

"What are you doing?" he asked, stilling her hand.

"I want to see you," she admitted.

"And do what?" He chuckled, ripping open

the last of the buttons and freeing himself. His cock jumped free, jutting up against his stomach, and it was her turn to wet her lips.

"Do you even know what can be done?" he asked, stroking his cock with his hand in long, slow strokes.

Reign shook her head, having no idea, but she was starting to wonder if what she was imagining was possible. "No, but I'm certain you will tell me, will you not?"

His eyes darkened further, and his breathing increased. "Some women will take a man into their mouth. Kiss his length, stroke it with their tongue, suckle it to drive the man mad with desire."

Reign's imaginings had been correct, and the thought of doing that to Bellamy, having him in her total control, was an elixir she could not deny herself.

"Will you let me?" She wiggled closer, pushing his hand off his manhood and replacing it with hers. "Let me take you into my mouth, Bellamy. I want to give you as much pleasure as you have afforded me."

He made a deep, gravelly sound that made her blood sing. "I would enjoy that very much, but I will not force you. Only if you truly want to."

Reign nodded, moving closer still. "Oh, I want to," she said.

She leaned down, kissing the purple head of his manhood. It jumped against her lips, and she smiled before licking the small droplet of pearl-colored liquid that pooled on its tip.

Salty but not unpleasant.

"Oh, dear God," Bellamy groaned, clasping the squabs, his knuckles white. Was what she was about to do so powerful that it would leave him so distracted?

A heady thought indeed.

Without wasting another moment, she took the head of his penis into her mouth, suckling it.

"Reign," he moaned, his hand coming about her neck, his fingers spiking into her hair and sending a multitude of pins to the carriage floor.

She suckled harder, moving to take him farther into her mouth before she fell into a rhythm that suited them both. His manhood grew, stiffened into her mouth, and she teased him, laved, and blew on his member before stroking it with her hand.

Her ministrations seemed favorable. Bellamy lay his head against the squabs, his eyes closed, his breathing uneven and quick.

"I love pleasing you." Reign increased her pace, taking him deeper still, working him with her mouth and her hand, wanting to make him come undone as he had made her in his lap with his hand.

The idea that what he had done with his

hand could also be done with his mouth made dampness pool between her legs, and she squeezed them together, wanting him, even now when she was determined to make him unravel in her mouth.

"Reign," he moaned, pumping into her mouth. "I'm close."

"Mmmm," she murmured, not stopping her assault.

"Ah fuck," he swore, as hot, gushing liquid spilled into her mouth. Whatever Reign was expecting, it was not what happened, but even so, she was delighted to have made him unravel in her arms just as she had hoped.

NINETEEN

"My turn," he all but growled, scooping Reign off her knees to place her on the squabs before him. This time it was his privilege to make her come, to find pleasure.

On his mouth.

He shuffled up her dress, pooling it at her waist. He wrenched her to the side of the seat, giving him what he needed to bring her pleasure, to drink in and savor every delicious thing about his wife-to-be.

She watched him, a wicked, curious light in her eyes, and he pushed her legs wider, hoisting them atop his shoulders so he could revel in her taste.

"You are unscrupulous, Bellamy," she breathed, biting her lip. Her hand slid through his hair, pushing it off his face, and he threw her a

look that promised retribution for the utter pleasure she had wrought upon him.

"You have no idea, my darling." He dipped
his head, kissing along her legs, taking turns with
each to ensure both were well loved. Her cunny
glistened with need and he ran his fingers across
her sex, teasing her, taunting her.

Hell, he wanted to taste her.

She moaned, wiggled closer and he smirked.
"You'll enjoy this, I promise," he said, dipping his
head. He laved her sex, taunting her nubbin with
his tongue, flicking and sucking it in turn.

She gasped, undulating against his mouth,
and desire rippled through him for a second time.
His cock hardened, more than ready to take her,
to fuck them both to oblivious bliss.

"You taste as sweet as honeyed wine," he said,
increasing his strokes, his lashings against her sex.

"Bellamy," she gasped. "This is madness, but I
adore it. I want more."

He grinned and pushed her toward the pin-
nacle he enjoyed most. A woman coming apart
from his mouth was the most exquisite sight and
sound a man could ever enjoy. She grew wetter
still, her movements bold and fierce, and he knew
she was not far from orgasm.

"Yes, Bellamy," she gasped, her body seeking
release, heedless of anything else.

He ate her, laved and kissed her, suckled and
enjoyed wringing out every last ounce of satisfac-

tion she could have. Her moan and soft sighs of delight filled him with joy, music to his ears.

"I want you," she said, clasping the lapels of his coat and hoisting him toward her. She kissed him hard, their tongues tangling in a dance of desire.

Bellamy pushed his breeches farther down his legs and sank deep into her cunny. They moaned in unison. The sensation of being in her, her wet, tight cunny taunting him, was too much.

He took her, pumped into her with relentless strokes as the carriage rumbled along the road. She wrapped her legs around his hips and held on to him, took what he gave her, and they lost themselves in the sensation of each other.

"You're so beautiful," he said. "I want you. Always. I've always wanted you and no other."

She threw back her head and screamed his name as her core spasmed about his cock, wrenching his release along with hers. He kissed her screams away and muffled their moans of ecstasy so no one would hear.

For several minutes they stayed entwined before he slumped onto the seat, adjusting his breeches. Reign sat beside him, pushing down her gown and attempting to fix her hair as best she could.

She looked over to him, her cheeks red and a wicked, naughty grin on her lips.

He leaned forward and kissed her softly. "I

want you even now," he said, meaning every word.

Her eyes glazed over with delight. "Tonight at the inn you will have me. I will not deny you anything. You know that."

That he knew indeed.

———

THEY MADE LONDON THE FOLLOWING afternoon, and after bidding Reign goodbye at Lord and Lady Chilsten's London home, Bellamy traveled to his town house on Brook Street, ready for a bath and new attire.

He strode into his library, needing to pen some missives before retiring for the night. His steward needed to be informed of his impending marriage, along with his London household.

He flicked through the invitations that had arrived since he was away and carefully picked the events he would attend. He needed the upper echelon of society to accept his marriage and they would, he would ensure that was so.

He would also host a ball to announce the betrothal and soon. The quicker they were married, the better it would be for them all and would suppress any murmurings of Reign's employment at his estate.

Forget what people think, as Reign says. Just live for yourself.

Bellamy tossed the last few invitations into the bin, those unsuitable to his needs, and ran a hand through his hair. The thought of anything halting him from marrying Reign made his blood run cold.

Tomorrow evening when they attended Lord and Lady Lawrence's ball, he would ensure Chilsten and Reign were given admittance had they not received an invite already. It would be an adequate night to judge how the *ton* would react to their courting.

Most would have known how he felt when she had debuted in 1807, and some may have felt sorry for them both after what transpired, but others would not. He had been caught in a compromising position, after all, and had lost any possibility of marrying the woman he wanted.

The woman he loved …

He sighed, knowing to his very core that the emotional response to Reign was true. His being here in the middle of the Season was proof of that. He would fight to have her accepted, to protect her name due to circumstances out of her control.

And circumstances his own inability to keep away from her had placed her in too.

Because he loved her, and nothing was too much for Reign.

. . .

THE LAWRENCE'S BALL WAS A CRUSH, AND Bellamy took Reign's hand before entering the house, placing it firmly on his arm. She was a vision tonight in her shimmering, golden gown. Her hair was up in an abundance of curls and jewels, no doubt borrowed from her good friend the Marchioness of Chilsten.

He could not take his eyes off her. So beautiful, regal, and elegant to the beholder. Anyone seeing her would never imagine that only a week ago, she was his daughter's governess, her gowns much less stylish.

Shame washed over him that he had allowed his fear to keep her in that position instead of proposing to her the moment she had reentered his life.

"You look utterly breathtaking, my darling. You will be the belle of the ball this evening," he said, pulling her close, wishing she did not wear long, white silk gloves that stopped him from being able to feel her, touch her as he wanted.

She grinned, her cheeks kissed by a rosy hue. "Why thank you, kind sir," she said, a teasing note in her voice. "Let us hope my attire and company are suitable enough to keep the gossip from shredding my reputation as a fraud."

He frowned, not liking her self-derogatory remark. "We will not allow you to be tarnished merely because you attended my house party and then could not include yourself as much as you like." He winked at her, and she chuckled.

"They know I was not there as a guest. I think this is a mistake, Bellamy."

He could feel her tremble under his hold, and he patted her hand, wanting to comfort her. "Marrying you, playing this game is no mistake. We will make them think they were wrong all along, and they are not bright enough to imagine otherwise. Do not forget we have dukes and viscounts, not to mention a marquess on our side, myself included. They will not naysay our story."

Speaking of all the titled friends he had rallied for assistance, they entered the ball and spied most of them congregated near the terrace doors.

"You see," he said, dipping his head toward their allies. "All the Woodville ladies and their husbands are in attendance along with the Yorks. The *ton* holds no chance of winning this war. They ought to relent immediately and raise their white flags."

"I do hope you're right," she said as they stepped in the direction of their friends and comrades-in-arms.

TRUE TO HIS WORD AND MUCH TO Reign's surprise, the ball was enjoyable. Nary an eyebrow was raised in her direction when the *ton* noticed the acceptance and loving response she had gained from her old friends in Grafton, now ladies who ruled the *ton*, having married so high in society.

She, too, she supposed, would join their ranks in a month when she became Lady Lupton-Gage, a dream she had never thought would ever happen.

"Will you dance with me?" Bellamy asked her, bending over her hand.

Without hesitation, she accepted and let him lead her onto the floor for a waltz. "Do you need to ask me, my lord?" she chuckled as he pulled her into his arms, holding her closer than what was proper. "Careful, or you'll cause a scandal," she teased.

He shook his head, but she saw that he found her comment amusing. "I'm trying to be more like you, Miss Hall. Not so fearful of scandal, maybe I should embrace it more if it enables me to marry a woman as sweet and wonderful as you are."

Had she been ice, she would have melted at his words. She took him in, all his handsomeness, and wondered how she had become so fortunate. How had she been so lucky to have ended up at his estate when she could have been sent to any place in England for employment?

"I'm glad you think so, for I feel the same, my lord." Reign wanted to tell him, to admit that her feelings had always tittered on the edge, leaning more toward love than mere like, but she did not.

He had not said it to her, after all.

"You should have always been mine," he murmured, leaning close, so near that for a scandalous moment, she thought he may kiss her on the dance floor in front of all the *ton*.

The thought sent a thrill through her.

"I've always been yours too, Bellamy," she admitted. The truth of her words no longer needed to be concealed, pushed down where they did not hurt so much every day she lived without him. "Even during all the years I lived in Grafton, hundreds of miles from you, lost to you, my heart only belonged to you," she admitted.

"Had you not manifested at my estate that day, I would have come for you, Reign. I know I would not have been able to live without you forever. Even if our courtship were considered scandalous, I would not have been unable to deny us forever."

She slipped her arm farther about his shoulder, holding him near. "My knight, coming to rescue me. I would have waited even when Mr. Johnson from two doors down from my cottage in Grafton could not alter my mind in marriage. I may have lost you, but I wanted you still."

"A Mr. Johnson proposed? You did not tell me that before," he queried, a small frown between his brows.

She remembered the day she had been sitting outside in her front garden, wondering if the carrots she had planted were ready for harvesting. "His proposal was much less interesting than yours, my lord. He did not get down on his knees as you did." She shrugged. "I could not accept."

"My proposal was most memorable indeed," he agreed, his eyes darkening in need. "Come with me. I want to be alone with my betrothed."

Reign glanced about and noted there were some eyes upon them. "We cannot. People will talk even more, and we do not want to make any gossip for them," she declared.

He paused for a moment before letting go of her hand. "Meet me in the hall just outside that door in ten minutes. I shall be waiting." Without another word, he turned on his heel and was gone.

Reign left the dance floor and found Julia standing alongside a group of gentlemen, her husband included. Their discussion about horses growing livelier with each minute.

"Where has Lupton-Gage disappeared to?" Julia asked her, watching her keenly.

Reign fought to keep her features from revealing the wicked imaginings that were floating through her mind but failed. Her friend tsk-tsked her, shaking her head. "Behave, my dear," she warned her.

"He has gone to get some air, I believe. He

will be back soon," she lied, turning her attention to the dancing instead.

"You're a terrible liar, and the reason I know you're lying is that I have been in your situation and know what the marquess is about," she said, a small lift to her lips as if she were not so disapproving.

"I cannot wait to be his wife. I feel like I have postponed a lifetime to be by his side again. To know there are no impediments to our union. The next four weeks cannot pass soon enough for me."

Julia brushed her arm, smiling. "I know you do, and I'm so very happy for you. And selfishly of me, I'm happy for me too, for I shall see more of you and you will no longer be able to deny my invitations. I have missed you terribly," she said.

"I have missed you as well," Reign admitted. "We shall have a jolly good time in London next Season, both of us married and happy." Reign waited for the end of the dance before she made her excuses. "I shall return momentarily. I'm in need of the retiring room."

"Of course you are," Julia replied, her tone one of disbelief. "Enjoy yourself," she added just when Reign had stepped away.

She chuckled, unable to hide her delight, before leaving the ballroom to find her betrothed.

How well that sounded.

TWENTY

Bellamy paced the darkened passage that only held the smallest light from the closed ballroom door and the window at the end of the hall.

The patter of slippered feet on the parquetry floor caught his attention, and he leaned against the wall, hoping it was Reign coming to join him.

Already it felt like an age since he had seen her last. Too long.

That he could not function without her, could not go a day without wondering where she was or what she was doing, told him that a lifetime without her would never have sufficed.

His words to her earlier tonight were as true as him standing here. He adored everything about her and loved her dearly.

She was his soulmate.

An elegant figure, one he knew intimately, came around the corner, and he breathed a relieved breath that she had come. "I had started to fear you would not join me," he admitted, stealing a kiss.

She wrapped her arms around his waist, and he loved how comfortable she was with him, how a husband and wife ought to be.

"Julia is on to us, I believe. I do not think she thought I was using the retiring room at all. In fact, I'm surprised she did not ask to come with me and halt me from coming to join you."

Bellamy threw back his head and laughed. Reign reached up, placing her finger over his lips, silencing him. "Bellamy, someone will hear and come to see why you're giggling."

He pulled her close, tipping his head to lean his forehead against hers. "Well, should they come, they would find a besotted man. A man who has regained the love of his life after too many years living without her. A man who will never let her go again."

He had said it. Finally. And the realization filled her heart with joy.

The vision of Bellamy began to blur as tears pooled in her eyes. She sniffed, having wondered and hoped that he loved her. That he would declare himself before their wedding.

"I love you too," she said, leaning forward and

kissing him softly. "And I missed you. Terribly so."

He stepped back and tugged her toward a door that led away from the ballroom. The room was as dark as the hall, the curtains drawn aside, and no fire or candles were alight.

The door closed, encasing them in their little, secluded space, just as she preferred. The idea of days and weeks ahead, being able to sit with each other late into the evenings, to have dinner and sleep beside Bellamy every night filled her with delight.

She could not wait to be the Marchioness of Lupton-Gage.

No more sneaking off to be alone like they were now.

No sooner was she in the room did he pull her into his arms, kissing her with a fierceness that left her breathless and grappling for purchase.

"I do not like you living with Lord and Lady Chilsten. I want you under my roof. Four weeks is too long away," he said.

She nodded, pulling him back to kiss her more. The time for talking was over. Need thrummed through her, and heat pooled at her core. Now that she had been introduced to the delights of bedding Bellamy, she knew what she wanted.

And when she wanted it.

He walked her backward until she came up against the door. He hoisted up her dress, lifting her against his waist. She locked her legs about his back, wanting him as much as he wanted her.

A thrill ran through her.

"You make me lose control," he growled. "We should not be here. We could be caught at any moment, and yet, I have to have you."

"Yes," she agreed. He reached between them, ripping his falls open, taunting her sex with his hand.

She moaned when he thrust into her, taking her with impressive ability. "Bellamy," she gasped, accepting him, all of him.

She would never get enough, not even if they had been married for a million years. One lifetime was too short.

BELLAMY PUMPED INTO REIGN, TOOK HER with a savage need that he ought not, but living without her for two days, missing her, wanting her, it had been too long.

Not that she seemed to mind his fierce taking of her against a door. Dear God, she was tight, wet, and made the sweetest sounds each time he thrust into her cunny.

He kissed her hard, suckling her tongue, losing himself in the feel of her willing and pliant body. How had he kept away from her? How had he allowed himself to fall into a void of fear over what others would think if he followed his heart and married the untitled country lass from Grafton?

The moment he found out his wife had died, he should have gone for her, married her, and been happy for years.

"Bellamy," she sighed, undulating against him in a way that made his balls tighten.

He was close, and the need to spend and make her increase with a child overrode any caution he had before marriage.

"Come for me," he demanded of her, thrusting hard, giving her what they both wanted.

She threw back her head, her fingers spiking into his shoulders as her orgasm ripped through her. Her cunny convulsed about his cock, drawing him closer still. He fucked her and rode out her pleasure before spilling his seed, her gasps and moans of delight searing into his mind.

For several minutes they stayed against the door. He kissed her with exquisite slowness, drinking in her embrace before settling her onto her feet.

He glanced at Reign and grinned at the starry-eyed vixen he was about to marry. A woman who was not fearful of him, his love, or how he liked to fuck.

He was the luckiest bastard in the world.

. . .

THEY RETURNED TO THE BALL. BELLAMY ignored the marchioness's appraising, if not knowing, look she bestowed on them both.

The marchioness most certainly knew what they had been up to during the half hour they were absent from the ball, but he did not care. He did not care who knew of his affection for the woman at his side. He would marry Reign, announce the betrothal at his ball one week from today and celebrate the happy event to the fullest.

He procured two glasses of champagne from a passing footman before handing one to Reign. "To us," he whispered, unable to take his eyes from her beauty and her thoroughly kissed mouth.

Even now, he desired her. Would this affliction be with him always? Something told him it would be.

"Reign," he said, turning to her. "Let us not wait for my ball. Why do we not announce our engagement this evening if Lord and Lady Lawrence approve? There is no reason why we should not. My daughter knows of our intention, and that is all I care about knowing first. What are your thoughts?" he asked her.

Her eyes flew wide before she smiled, nodding. "Yes, let us, and then it does not matter if you show more interest in me than any other. We shall not have to be so circumspect."

"I agree," he said. "I will announce it now. Wait here."

Without further ado, he moved through the throng of guests. He soon located Lord and Lady Lawrence and spoke to them for several minutes. His request brought on a multitude of congratulations. Bellamy made his way up to where the orchestra played for the evening. He leaned on the railing that overlooked the ballroom floor and whistled, gaining everyone's attention.

They turned and looked up at him. Low murmurings and curious looks stared back.

"Lords, ladies and gentlemen, I have an announcement to make," he said, finding his betrothed and smiling at Reign. "I'm delighted to tell you all that I have asked Miss Reign Hall to be my wife, my future Marchioness of Lupton-Gage, and she has accepted. Congratulate us," he shouted, lifting his glass of champagne.

Compliments rang out, and he moved back to join Reign, who was also inundated with people wanting to wish them happy.

Why he had not done this sooner, he would never know. The *ton* had not mentioned Reign's humble past years, nor would they, now she was to be a marchioness.

"Thank you for all your kind words," he

stated, more than pleased with the reaction of the *ton*.

That the majority of the guests seemed accepting was good enough for him, and he would stop worrying his daughter would be impacted further by scandal.

All was right in the world, and the future was bright.

"Bellamy," a familiar voice from his past murmured at his side. He turned and watched, disbelievingly, as a familiar ghost from the past pushed back her hood and smiled at him.

He stared, unable to comprehend who was standing before him.

"Sally?" His question came out strained, and he cleared his throat. He shook his head, certain he must be mistaken. "No, it cannot be," he said, unwilling to believe that the one woman who had made him lose everything was standing before him, smirking like the evil, conniving witch she had always been.

He heard Reign gasp and step back from him, and the thought that he would lose her again because of the woman before him sent panic through his blood.

"Good evening, my darling husband. Have you missed me?" she asked him.

He gaped. Had she truly asked him such a question? "I beg your pardon, madam, " he said, unable to comprehend what was happening. She was alive? Living abroad all these years without a care with a multitude of different suitors.

Lovers.

A large spot on her neck became visible when she turned to the *ton*, and he knew it was a love mark, and a new one if he were any judge. Fellow guests watched on with eager, hungry eyes as to what was happening before them. A kink in the night they had not expected.

She turned back to him, linking her arm with his and smiling at everyone before them. "I have returned from abroad. My darling husband was misinformed of my death two years ago, but I have found my way back to his side." She turned to Reign standing beside Lady Chilsten, the marchioness's wide, shocked eyes nothing compared to the horror, the devastation written across his betrothed.

He had hurt her again.

Damn his wife to hell for all the pain she caused.

"I'm so terribly sorry, Miss Hall, but it seems you shall miss out yet again on marrying Lord Lupton-Gage, but," his wife stated, gesturing to the throng of guests, "I'm certain that there are gentlemen here more than willing to marry a plain country mouse such as yourself. God knows you have waited long enough for a proposal. What are you now, seven and twenty?" The marchioness tapped her chin in thought, evil glee sparkling in her cold eyes. "Well, perhaps there are not. It is unlikely you could bear children at your senior age. Which brings me to ask, how is our daughter, Bellamy? I have missed little Alice so very much."

"Have a pleasant evening, my lord, Lady Lupton-Gage," he heard Reign state at his side before she fled.

He went to follow her, but a stilling hand from Lord Chilsten halted his steps. "Not now, Gage. We shall expect you tomorrow," he said, glaring at Sally before following his wife and Reign as they made their way out the door.

Bellamy ground his teeth, turning to his wife. "Home. Now."

TWENTY-ONE

T hankfully the stable lads working the carriages at the Lawrence's ball quickly secured his carriage, and they were soon ensconced and heading back to Brook Street.

Bellamy remained quiet as they had left the ball, but the moment the carriage lurched forward, he knew he could stay silent no longer.

"What do you think you're doing? You're supposed to be dead. We had a memorial erected at Davion Hall for you. Your daughter grieved your loss. How is it that you've been alive these two years and thought it appropriate to reveal yourself this evening? Of all evenings to be so cruel, you choose the one when I'm finally rid of you and moving forward with my life."

She laughed, but there was no mirth in the sound. For a woman who looked like an angel dropped from the sky, nothing but evil wickedness flowed through her veins. He had long forgotten how cruel and cold his wife could be, but here it was, before him yet again and with the ability to crush his dreams of finally being happy.

Of marrying the woman he loved.

The thought of losing Reign again made his hands fist at his sides.

She waved his words aside as if they did not matter, and he supposed that was the most genuine part of his wife. She had never cared what anyone thought so long as she was allowed to do as she wished.

Which she did, much to the near ruination of her family.

"Do not be so dramatic, Bellamy. You were always one to worry about what others thought ... well, you certainly were after you married me." She inspected her gown for a moment. "I suppose I did like to live life as I pleased, and fucking other men pleased me very well. Do you know," she said, chuckling. "I do not even know if Alice is yours. How funny is that?"

A cold chill ran down his spine and he fought not to cast up his accounts. To think his precious Alice was not his was impossible. She had his family traits. He would not allow her to taunt him with such heinous imaginings.

"You lie to hurt me for reasons I will never understand, but even if that were not the case, she is my daughter. I raised and loved her when you would not. She is mine, even in the unlikely chance that she does not share my blood."

She shrugged, leaning toward the window to glance over the Mayfair streets. "I do hope Miss Hall is not so very glum. I know she wanted to marry you all those years ago. Such a shame it was not her in the room that night, but instead me. Your life would have been so much less complicated had you not been so gullible and, should I say, cock hard for the little chit from Grafton."

It took all of Bellamy's strength to remain where he was and not strangle his wife. She was so cruel and had become even more caustic since she had left England. Not that she was ever very nice. She had set out to get what she wanted, access to his money and the security of his title, and that was all. Everyone else be damned.

"Do not mention Miss Hall's name in my presence. You do not have the right to speak of her. Not here or anywhere else in the world. Do I make myself clear?"

She chuckled. "I suppose I should make plans to return to the Lake District. As boring as it is way up there, but still, that is my home, and I'm the lady of the house."

His stomach churned at the thought of such truth, and he swallowed, fighting the urge to cast up his accounts. "You are not the lady of the house, nor have you ever wished to be."

"Ah, but I am," she said, interrupting him.

"And I shall take up my place in society, and there is nothing you can do about it." She studied him, a smirk across her lips. He studied her and noted the heavy paste upon her face that gave her complexion a healthier glow than it truly had.

Was she ill? Had she caught some disease while abroad? Or had her hard lifestyle merely caught up with her?

"Do not forget, my lord, that you dislike scandal, and if you make trouble for me or deny me my right as your wife, hazards will impact our darling daughter." She pouted, and he had never seen anything more false. "And we would not like that, now would we?" she said, turning back to look out onto the streets, laughing at nothing he saw that was amusing.

The woman was mad.

But worse, what would he do? What could he do?

He ran a hand through his hair, his mind frantically thinking. The night had started so well, with so much promise and celebration. How could happiness yet again be ripped from him and Reign?

God damn it all to hell. What was he going to do?

REIGN PACED ABOUT HER BEDROOM, forcing herself to take deep, calming breaths. She swiped at her cheeks, hating that her eyes would not stop leaking.

"Reign, please come and sit and have tea with me. It will make you feel better," Julia said, her voice pleading and comforting, but nothing she could say or do would make the situation any better.

Lady Lupton-Gage was still alive, and she had just been betrothed publicly to his lordship before all the *ton*. If rumors of her working as a governess were not bad enough, now she would be known as a scarlet woman.

"People will think that I knew her ladyship was alive and that I chose to betroth myself to Lord Lupton-Gage. I'm ruined, Julia. You ought to send me away right now. I don't know where. I have nowhere to go." She slumped onto the settee beside Julia and stared at the fire.

The truth of her situation crashed down on her. "I do not even have a home. And although I came into some funds, they are not enough without employment. I shall have to find work elsewhere and quickly. Or book passage to America and leave and hope I find work as soon as I reach the new world."

"You are not going anywhere, even if I have to make you my companion to stop you from panicking. Until then, you are my best friend staying with me for the Season and had the unfortunate luck to betroth yourself to a man all of us thought widowed for several years."

Reign rubbed her brow. An annoying ache that she knew would soon turn into a headache. Her stomach churned, and she swallowed hard the lump in her throat that made composure difficult.

The urge to scream, to declare everything was unfair in her life bore against her, but she resisted. There was little point. Nothing could change the fact that the marchioness was alive and well and had been living abroad all these years under the assumption she was not.

Why the Marchioness of Lupton-Gage had wanted to live under such a ruse was beyond her, but as true as it was that she sat before her oldest friend, her ladyship was right at this minute sharing a house with the man she loved.

"Her ladyship seems to win, no matter what. I cannot believe it is true. Not again, Julia."

Julia reached out and clasped her hand, her brow furrowed in concern. "Lord Lupton-Gage will make it right. I'm sure of it," Julia said, but even to Reign's ears, her friend's declaration rang false.

There was nothing that could be done. They were married. Having lived apart or not, she was back, very much alive and ready to be the marchioness once again from all accounts.

"Bellamy will not do anything to harm his

daughter's future. He will tolerate the marchioness, and I shall go home. If I could go home." Reign fumbled in her gown to find her handkerchief and, unable to find one, wiped her nose on the back of her hand, bedamning etiquette.

"I'm in love with him, Julia. Whatever am I going to do?" she asked her friend, the world she had thought was hers to take crumbling around her.

Julia came and sat beside her, pulling her into a tight embrace. The affection was the last straw that Reign could endure, and she sobbed, the tears falling freely, her ability to speak wrenched from her for several minutes.

Julia held her tight, rubbing her back. "Let us see what Lord Lupton-Gage has to say tomorrow when he calls. He will need to explain what all of this is about and what he is going to do."

Reign nodded but did not naysay her friend. There was nothing for him to do, nothing for her to do either. Lady Lupton-Gage had won a second time, regarding their love, and that was all there was about the situation.

Now she would have to learn to live with seeing them together until she decided what she should do in her life.

Wherever that journey took her.

TWENTY-TWO

Bellamy paced the parlor that Lord and Lady Chilsten had offered him to discuss last night's events with Reign.

He heard light footsteps on the parquetry floor and stilled, holding his hands behind his back in preparation for facing his betrothed.

His love.

Reign stepped into the room, and the pit of his stomach dropped. She was as pretty as she had always been, but her eyes, normally a handsome blue, were shadowed by fear and trepidation.

He stepped toward her, and she held out a hand, sitting instead on a single settee beside the unlit fire, a sure sign she wanted to keep him at a distance.

"You wished to see me, Lord Lupton-Gage?" she stated, meeting his eyes quickly before she glanced back toward the hearth.

He came around the settee and sat as close as he could to her. "Look at me, Reign," he pleaded. "I did not mean for this to happen. Please do not punish me with coldness when nothing has changed for me."

She shook her head, not meeting his eyes. "But everything has changed, no matter how much we may both wish differently. Your wife is alive, a fact the *ton* will expect you to celebrate. I would suggest you change our betrothal ball at your home to celebrate her return, especially now that it's come to an end."

Bellamy fought the panic that rose within him. This could not happen again. He could not lose her once more.

"How can you think that I want this? That I want to remain married to a woman who has despised me from the moment we said 'I do'. I do not. I cannot live without you again, Reign."

"But you will have to," she cut in, her voice brooking no argument. "There is no choice, not for either of us." She met his eyes finally. "Your wife has not passed, and you will be expected to be happy over that fact, no matter how much you may regret me and what we have lost in the interim. I know you care for me, and I care for you, too. That has not changed. But our circumstances have, and we must adjust."

"Reign, I never loved her. She tricked me into marrying her—"

"It is done, Bellamy. As much as we may wish to change our past, it is already written in the pages of history. No matter the circumstances that brought upon your first marriage, all of it happened, and anything we shared was severed. That has happened again. Lady Lupton-Gage is alive, and that is everything anyone needs to know."

"It is not everything to me. She thinks life and emotions are a game. She enjoys playing with her victims. You must not go near her, not at any balls or parties where you may cross her path. She will not be kind. Promise me," he said, trying to salvage something from this horrid mess that his wife had created.

He closed his eyes. How he loathed that word, that term, when speaking of Sally.

"Lady Chilsten has been kind enough to allow me to stay here, and I shall until I decide what I will do. I will attempt to keep away from you and her ladyship. I do not want to see her any more than I want to see you with her."

"I do not love her, Reign," he vouched, kneeling before her and taking her hands. He frowned at the chill in her hands and tried to warm them with his. "I love you. I want you," he said, having never declared anything more true in his life. "I cannot imagine living without you again, and I do not want to."

She met his eyes, hers swimming with tears.

"But we have to. There is no choice." She reached up and clasped his jaw. "My feelings remain unchanged, Bellamy. I love you too. I have always done so, but we both need to accept that we are not meant to be. The universe seems to know better than either of us and halts any attempts of us having happiness together. We need to part, to sever our contact to make the next few months and years as easy as possible."

Bellamy ignored her words, not willing to lose her, but then what choice did he have? He could not ask her to be his mistress. He would not denigrate what either of them felt of the other by asking such a thing. Even if that was the only way open for them he could see.

His wife was alive, and to divorce her would mean a tarnish against his name that his daughter would never live down.

"I do not know what to do," he admitted, lost for words or an out. How was he to live without the woman he loved? He had pushed aside his feelings for years but now had admitted to them, declared them to Reign, and did not want to smother them again.

"There is nothing that you can do, Bellamy. There is nothing that either of us can do," she said, leaning forward and kissing him. Her touch severed his soul in two. He could feel the kiss was a goodbye, a farewell that this time felt undeniably final.

There would not be another. When he left this house this morning, he would never return and see Reign waiting for him.

Just like their envisioned happy future, it would be ripped from them forever.

———

REIGN WALKED INTO LORD CHILSTEN'S library the following morning and found Julia with her husband, looking at her expectantly. "Come, sit," Julia said, a warm smile on her face.

Her friend had been the epitome of comfort these past days, and she did not know what she would have done without her. She had allowed her to cry on her shoulder and to vent when she needed. A truer friend she could not have asked for.

Reign sat, folding her hands in her lap, and wondered what this impromptu meeting was about.

"Reign, as you know, you came into an inheritance from your late uncle. One whom you did not know," Lord Chilsten informed her.

She nodded, having already expected this information to arise now that she was in London, and since it had been some weeks since his passing. "Yes, that is right. I was informed of his passing before we left Derbyshire, but there were few details at that stage as to what I would inherit. I believe the sum to be a hundred pounds or thereabouts," she said, hoping that was still true. It would certainly help her not feel so dependent on her friends until she left.

"Well, yes, that is partially true. There is a hundred pounds coming, but there was an error on the missive that reached Lupton-Gage, and the actual sum you and your distant cousins will be receiving each is ten thousand pounds."

"Excuse me?" Reign stuttered. She clasped her chest, sure her heart was about to beat out of her body. "That cannot be right. He could not have been so generous, surely?" she asked, laughing at her question and the absurdity of it.

"It is indeed true, Reign. You're an heiress and independent from this day forward. I know it does not repair what was between you and Lupton-Gage, but you are no longer dependent on anyone. You may do as you wish, maybe find love once more and marry."

"Or I could be happy on my own, back in my cottage in Grafton, if I can purchase it back," she said, the idea of returning to her small village, hiding away and allowing her heart to heal more tempting than anything else.

"Or you could do that," Lord Chilsten agreed, his smile full of pity.

And that was the crux of staying here in London. Everyone would look at her with pity except for Lady Lupton-Gage, who would be as smug as she had been during their coming out year.

"Would you like me to see if you can purchase your cottage back?" his lordship asked her. "It may not be too late."

Hope, an emotion she had not felt in several days, ran through her, and she nodded. "Please, if you would. I would be most grateful. Returning to Grafton will allow me to heal and gather my thoughts. I'm not certain what the future holds, but I know it does not include marriage to Bellamy."

"Oh, Reign," Julia cooed, coming over to her and wrapping her arm about her shoulders. "Time will heal your wound."

Reign glanced up at her friend, knowing Julia meant well, but the words held little comfort. They grated upon her, taunted her, and hurt her more than she could say, knowing how false they were. That her life was not as she had wished it. "If you were to lose Lord Chilsten, would your heart heal, Julia?" she asked her, patting her friend's hand on her shoulder.

Julia stared at her, and Reign could see that she did not need to answer the question to know what she thought. "I think I shall return to my room. I'm terribly tired. It has been a long two days."

"We shall see you at dinner," Lord Chilsten

said, empathy still shadowing his gaze whenever it lighted on her.

Reign nodded. "Thank you, yes," she said, leaving them alone. A way of life she, too, would need to get used to, for she would never marry now. That dream was lost to her just as Bellamy was.

Twenty-Three

Reign had been able to avoid Bellamy for the week after their betrothal announcement, which had ended with Lady Lupton-Gage returning from the dead to ruin all her hopes.

She supposed she could not blame the woman for wanting to return to England and try to salvage some of her past, but the thought of her being under the same roof as Bellamy left a cold ache where her heart used to beat.

She missed him. Wanted him still, married as he was, and tonight at his ball, which had once been meant for them and their happiness, was now in celebration of Lady Lupton-Gage's return.

All of society would be there, if only to watch the games afoot regarding the marchioness. Reign had little doubt the woman would heed the advice and remain chaste and proper. She had never done so before in her marriage, and Reign knew she would not start now.

Poor Bellamy would have to try to keep up with her to smother any scandals the woman would cause all over town.

Reign entered the ballroom with Lord and Lady Chilsten, who had recommended she attend, if only to show publicly she had not meant to cause strife between the marquess and his wife by becoming betrothed to him when she was still alive. Reign held her head high, not wanting to be pitied for the rest of her life.

"You will do wonderfully, Reign. I know tonight will be difficult for you," Julia said yet again, possibly for the tenth time already this evening. "But we shall be by your side."

Reign smiled, trying to put her friend at ease, who seemed more nervous than she was. "Truly, I shall have to face them eventually if I'm to stay in town. I have nothing to be ashamed of. I did not know she was alive, and nor did Lord Lupton-Gage. Much better to find out now instead of after our wedding night."

Julia gasped, covering her mouth with her silk-covered hand. "Do not even say such a thing. You would have been ruined for sure had such an occasion occurred, even if it were not your fault."

"Life is unfair, and more so for the female

sex," Lord Chilsten drawled as they moved through the throng.

"I'm so sorry to hear of your broken betrothal," Miss Fernly said as she passed.

"We do hope you're able to find a match soon, Miss Hall," another young lady called out, a snicker in her tone.

Reign inwardly sighed. She knew tonight would not be easy, but already it had started off harder than she thought. To be here, to be the one woman in the *ton* who had loved and lost the same man twice and to the same woman, was not ideal.

But at least you know he loved you as you loved him.

That was true, but it did not make losing him any easier. A ruckus started at the ballroom doors, and she turned to see Lady Lupton-Gage entering the ball, but not on her husband's arm.

Instead, a man of similar dishevelment to her ladyship walked alongside. His clothing splashed and stained with drink and food.

"What on earth ..." she heard Julia state, who came to stand at her side, her mouth all but gaping.

Reign glanced about the room and noted almost everyone present, too, was watching the spectacle stumble her way through the crowd. She gestured to some and spoke to others, her words cutting and cordial in equal measures.

What was wrong with the woman?

Reign took a calming breath and steeled herself when her ladyship spotted her, dragging her companion with her as she turned in her direction.

"Miss Hall, how surprising to see you here this evening. Have you not had enough yet of your heart being broken? You must wish to torture yourself seeing me happily back at my husband's side. A man only last week who was betrothed to ..." she stated, her high-pitched laugh not at all amusing. Not to Reign in any case.

She swallowed the bile that rose in her throat and took a step back when Lady Lupton-Gage's companion sneered and took a menacing step in her direction.

"We are all pleased you were not harmed, as we were informed. Lord Lupton-Gage would never have offered marriage to me had he known you were alive," she stated, loud enough for everyone to hear. "I wish you very happy."

Her ladyship scoffed, pinching her companion when he did not understand her sarcasm and react to her retort. "You do no such thing. You have loved his lordship for years. Pathetic, really," she drawled, pursing her lips, as if she had to study Reign for a minute or two. "But I knew from the moment he proposed that you would be heartbroken. Poor little Miss Hall, and poor you are."

Gasps sounded about them, and Reign fought to keep her composure. She would not make a scene. She would not be dragged into this sick, vile woman's world.

Instead, she did not say anything at all, which unfortunately seemed to increase Lady Lupton-Gage's ire tenfold.

"How providential it was that you were hired as a governess at my husband's home. Of all the estates and families in England, how was it that you ended up there, I wonder ..."

"I think we ought to leave," Lord Chilsten said just as Reign turned to see Bellamy making his way toward them, horror written across his handsome features.

Where had he been?

"I do not know what you mean," Reign stated, keeping to the story that they had all agreed upon when leaving Derbyshire.

Again, her ladyship laughed, the sound making Reign's teeth ache. "Oh, do be serious, child. Who do you think ensured your application for employment was directed to the Lupton-Gage estate?" She grinned, turning to everyone who listened about them. Their eyes wide, each leaning in as if the need to hear her ladyship's words were worth more than anything else in the world.

"I have always known, you see, that you loved his lordship but lost him to me, which of course, was what should have happened. A marquess marrying a nobody from Grafton, who ever heard of such a thing? But, I could not forgive your gumption, you see," she said, stumbling before righting herself.

"You are foxed, my lady," Julia declared, her tone ice. "Maybe you ought to retire."

People about them gasped but did not move. They merely turned toward Lady Lupton-Gage to see if she had a retort.

Her ladyship nodded. "Oh I am, Lady Chilsten. Why would I not be? This is a party, after all."

The guests chuckled, and Reign steeled her nerves to keep from scurrying away.

"Enough, Sally. I think it is time you retired before you embarrass yourself further," Lord Lupton-Gage said, coming to stand beside Reign.

She welcomed his presence and his strength and hoped that the ball would soon be rid of his wife. What a horrible woman she was. Who was this man she stood with anyway? Another lover to throw in her husband's face?

"All these years, and you never married. I have my spies who keep me informed, and I was not saddened to hear you had fallen on hard times. How very terrible for you, but how very fortunate for me. When you required a place as a governess, Derbyshire seemed the perfect solution, and you were so eager to start your new life. What fun it was to receive letters stating how you arrived, only to find my husband, the man you once hoped to marry, was your employer."

Reign gaped, and without a flicker of doubt, she knew who had been behind telling Lady Lupton-Gage of her triumph in getting her settled at that particular house. Mrs. Watkins had never been kind, no matter how much Reign had tried to be friendly to the housekeeper.

"How dare you, Sally," Bellamy seethed, glaring at his wife. Reign took a cautionary step back, having never heard his tone so deadly before. As if his words themselves could strike a person down.

"What is wrong with you that you would act so viciously toward anyone when you are so privileged? You live under the protection of my name. You tricked me into thinking that it was Miss Hall who would have been in that conservatory all those years ago to ensure I married you instead. You leave England for years. Abandoning your daughter and your marriage to rut about Europe with men such as the one who clings to your side even now."

The people about them all tittered at the marquess's damning words toward his wife. Ladies tipped up their noses at the marchioness's antics, the men shaking their heads in disgust.

It was Lady Lupton-Gage's turn to gape, and rightfully so; a surprisingly pink blush kissed the woman's cheeks. "How dare you insinuate anything about my character."

His lordship shrugged, meeting Reign's eyes a moment before turning back to his wife. "I will no longer pretend how you live your life is acceptable to me or our daughter. You flaunt your lovers, you taunt your equals, and you expect me to remain your forever loyal servant, well," he said, shaking his head. "I will no longer do it. The letter we received notifying us of your death, I believe you were behind. All a game to try to ensure that I was never able to find happiness. To bide your time until you could return to London, miraculously alive and ready to take up your mantle as marchioness when I did find love. You hated Miss Hall so very much that you kept this sick game of yours going for years, and to what end? To return, to laud it over her on the night we announced our engagement. And all because she was not as well-to-do as you. Not a child born of wealth and connections, but had the audacity to fall in love with one. A rich, titled marquess who loved her too."

Reign swallowed the lump in her throat and tried to blink her tears away, but they fell unheeded down her face. She had never heard Bellamy speak so, had never thought he would defend her so publicly or damn his wife in the same breath. But he was. Right at this moment, he had thrown all thought of scandal and what the *ton* may think aside to defend her honor, to defend their love, and she had never loved him more in her life.

TWENTY-FOUR

Bellamy knew he was possibly damning himself along with Reign and his wife with his public response to the marchioness's atrocious behavior. It was well beyond time that he said something. Time for him to throw all thoughts of what the people surrounding him at this very moment thought, and to hell with them all.

None of them mattered in any case. All that mattered was Reign and the life he wanted with her. And now he would ensure that that future did come to fruition. No matter the trouble or talk, his decision would undoubtedly ensue.

His wife glanced about the room, obstinate to her very core and possibly such a narcissist that she did not gauge the temperature of her actions and what people thought of her. She continued, "There is little you can do, Bellamy. I'm your wife, you may try to pack me off to Derbyshire, but I shall only travel again. Do as I please, as I always have. I fooled you for two years with false accounts in which all funds came to me. I'm a marchioness and far more intelligent than you give me credit for. My brother is a marquess, just as you are. They will never allow you to treat me with such little respect."

Bellamy gestured to the throng of guests. "Really?" he asked her. "And where is your family this evening? They were invited and did not attend. Do you truly believe they want to be associated with a woman of such loose morals as yourself? I know I no longer do and will not, from this very moment."

There, he had said, out loud and publicly, for everyone to hear. A weight that had settled on his shoulders lifted, and for the first time in many days, he felt ... hope.

Sally laughed again, and yet this time, the sound was as brittle as her reputation. "You cannot touch me, Bellamy. You have never had the stomach to be hard against anyone. In all the years of our marriage, you have never shown anyone that you have a backbone."

Her words stung, and he ground his teeth, not too proud to know that what she said was true. "I have been a coward. Always worried about what would affect our daughter and doing my best to keep her reputation intact with a mother of such loose morals as yourself. Your death upset her greatly. She mourned you, and yet all the while, you were alive and could have spared her that pain. You do not care for anyone, and I have, madam, this very evening, grown a backbone as you say, and I'm going to wield it like a sword. I'm going to divorce you. Come ruination or scandal, I'm going to rid myself of your presence, of any connection I have ever had in my life, and watch you sail off to your precious Europe and stay there."

Bellamy stepped over to where Reign stood, watching him in awe, and he took her hand, lifting her gloved fingers and kissing them. "I'm going to marry the woman I love. The woman who should have always been mine as I was hers. I'm going to marry Miss Hall, my daughter's wonderful governess, my friend of many years and who, the moment I saw her debut, has held my heart in the palm of her hands." He leaned down and kissed her lips, no longer willing to let anything or anyone come between what he wanted and how he wished to live his life. "Marry me, Reign," he asked her.

She bit her lip, her eyes wide. The room was eerily quiet, so much so one could hear a pin drop.

"You cannot marry that commoner. How absurd, and I shall fight you, Lupton-Gage. I shall fight you to remain your wife."

He rounded on Sally, stepping but an inch

from her face. "Why, when it is clear you have no wish to be my wife? You never have. And to be brutally honest, I loathed you from the moment you tricked me. That is no marriage I wish to be part of, and if you had any respect for yourself, your family, and your daughter, you would grant me what I want and be happy that I do not place you into an institution instead."

Reign's comforting hand slipped into his, and he clasped onto her tight. Needing her more than anything. He looked up, taking in all his guests. "The ball is now at an end, my lords and ladies. Please request your carriages," he said, striding past his wife and pulling Reign along with him.

He left the ballroom behind them, running into his butler in the foyer. "Have a maid pack everything of the marchioness and send it to Lord Perry's London home. She leaves immediately and is not to step past this foyer. Am I understood?" he demanded.

His butler nodded. "I shall ensure all is as you wish, my lord."

Bellamy continued toward the back of the house, needing to be alone with Reign. This evening, he had placed her in a position that he had not wanted, but he needed to know if she would remain by his side. Be his as he hoped after all that was about to occur between them and in their future life.

. . .

REIGN COULD BARELY KEEP UP WITH Bellamy as he rushed through his London home toward the back of the house. He strode through a large morning room that allowed the light from the eastern sky and out through the terrace doors into the gardens.

With quickened steps, they made their way down to a stone-and-glass pavilion overlooking a small lake.

"What are we doing here?" she asked him, stepping inside the opulent space that looked like it belonged to the main house and not in the extensive garden.

"I must know. I must hear from you if what I declared at the ball just now does not frighten you away. That you will marry me as I hope, no matter how long that may take."

Reign approached him, wrapping her arms around his waist and holding him close. He shivered in her arms. She knew the confrontation was something he deplored and in such a public manner had certainly caused him to shudder.

"I will wait for you, Bellamy. No matter how long or troublesome the next few months or years may be. I'm not going anywhere. You ought to know that of me by now. I waited for you even when you were lost to me in marriage. Even now, that I'm an heiress."

He frowned, pushing a few whisps of hair from her face. "An heiress. What are you talking of?"

She chuckled, leaning into his embrace. "Well, the one hundred pounds in the letter I received was in fact, ten thousand pounds. There was an error in the correspondence, but do you know what that means?" she asked him. "For us?"

He shook his head, pulling her closer still. "What?"

"It means that if you truly mean to divorce Lady Lupton-Gage, which you should know I fully respect and support, I can wait for you and not be a burden to anyone else in the interim. With her ladyship's antics, I do not think I shall have to wait long."

Bellamy sighed, running a hand through his hair and leaving it on end. Reign smiled, reached up, and settled it back down. "I will wait for you. No matter how long it takes. I shall return to Grafton. Lord Chilsten has already sent inquiries about purchasing back my cottage. I shall be there when you have settled things between yourself and Lady Lupton-Gage. I will not relent on my promise, for I love you so very much, Bellamy. So much that to see you tonight declare yourself so publicly, to defend your honor and the honor of your family, of that I could not have been more proud of you. For defending me," she said.

He lowered his head and kissed her. Hard.

She threw herself into the embrace, not knowing when she would see him again. It could be months, a year, or possibly more, but she would have one more night with him until then.

His kiss soothed the pain she knew she would endure being away from him. Their tongues danced, his hands everywhere, stripping them both of their clothes.

Reign forgot where they were or what had happened earlier. All that mattered was Bellamy. His hands, touch, and love were all for her and their future.

He tumbled them onto the settee, his heavy body covering hers, warming her in places she ached to fulfill. "I want you," she admitted, squirming beneath him, needing him with an appetite that would not be sated.

"I want you too. Always," he declared, helping her with her dress and ripping his falls open. Like two frantic people desperate for release, he joined with her, thrust into her, and took her as they wished.

"Bellamy," she cried out. He kissed her, smothering her words of longing that ripped from deep within her soul.

Their joining was full of madness, desperation, and love. So much love that it wrapped around her and gave her comfort. Sensation rippled, teased her senses, and she reveled in the feel of him, of having him with her, being hers from this day forward.

No matter what troubles tomorrow would bring, at least this night, they could have each other. A promise of better days ahead.

Reign wrapped her legs around his hips, and his stroke deepened, teasing her sensitive inner self, a place that ached for sweet release.

His hand kneaded her breast, rolling her nipple between his thumb and forefinger, and she gasped. So good. So brazen.

She would never get enough of him.

"I love you, Bellamy," she gasped as tremors rocked through her, coiling out to every part of her body and intoxicating her soul with delight.

She rode wave after wave of sheer bliss, clung to Bellamy as he pushed her forward and gave her what she wanted to the very sweet end. Only then did he join her, thrust hard into her cunny, spilling his seed deep into her womb.

"I love you too," he breathed against her lips, kissing her softly. "I promise you will not have to wait for me long."

She kissed him back, never doubting his word. "I know I shall not."

Epilogue

Four months later, Grafton

Reign lounged on the settee in her warm cottage. The scent of lamb cooking in the kitchen wafted through the house, reminding her of when she was a child.

After moving back to Grafton, she purchased new furnishings and repaired what needed fixing, along with a whole new wardrobe.

The snow fell heavily outside, and yet this year was so different from last. She was no longer cold or hungry or had to worry if her boots would make it to the local village to purchase what meager food she could afford.

Now she could buy whatever she needed, help her friends, and not be a burden to anyone.

"The paper, Miss Hall," her one and only maid said, placing *The Times* on the small table before her.

"Thank you," she said, reaching for it. Her stomach clenched, and she bolted upright at the headline on the front page. *Lady Lupton-Gage Dead from the Pox.* She gasped, quickly reading the article, and could not believe what was printed in black and white.

Bellamy's wife was dead?

She looked to see the date and noted it was already well over a week old. "Lizzie, has any mail come for me today?" she called out.

Her maid popped her head back into the parlor door. "No, Miss Hall. No mail for over a week now," she said before disappearing once more.

Reign bit her lip, wondering why Bellamy had not come for her. Had he changed his mind? Since leaving London four months ago, they had barely written, thinking it best since he was to start petitioning for a divorce. He could not be seen as an adulterer as well as his wife. Nothing would ever be finalized, then.

"Miss Hall?" Lizzie said, entering the room. "Lady Chilsten is here to see you."

Reign jumped to her feet, rushing out to the foyer to find Julia banging off her boots and wiping snow off her shawl.

"Julia," she shouted, pleasure flooding her at seeing her friend again. "It is so lovely to see you."

Julia pulled her into a quick embrace. "And I you, Reign. My visit is long overdue, but we're home for several days before returning to London."

Reign smiled, unable to believe her friend was standing before her again. "I have missed you. Tell me all your news?" she asked.

Julia studied her and nodded in approval. "Your dress is appropriate, so come. I have a surprise for you."

She looked past Julia and out the door where one could barely see through the snow. "A surprise? Outside?" she questioned, taking a cautionary step backward. The day was far too cold to venture outside.

Julia chuckled, picking up Reign's shawl that hung beside the door. "Yes, out there. Now come, I have a carriage waiting with hot bricks inside. You shall be warm enough," she said, and was once again striding toward the front gate.

Reign slipped on the shawl and bonnet and followed her friend. The carriage was indeed warm, and they were soon rolling toward the village.

"Will you tell me what this surprise is?" she asked.

"No," Julia smirked. "You will see soon enough." Reign glanced out the window and frowned as the carriage pulled up before the church.

"What are we doing here?" she asked.

Her friend tapped the side of her nose but

did not respond, and Reign's interest was piqued. A footman opened the door and helped them alight before Julia clasped her hand and walked toward the church doors.

They stepped into the foyer and her stomach twisted at the sight of Lord Chilsten. He approached her, bussing her cheeks and holding out his arm. "Shall we, Miss Hall?" he asked her, as mysterious as her friend was being.

Reign looked to Julia, who beamed before opening the doors to the church and revealing all the people waiting inside. Reign gasped at the sight of everyone. The Woodville girls she had played with as children stood, watching her, their smiles as genuine as the men who stood beside them. Mr. and Mrs. Woodville and several local friends had ventured out in the cold January afternoon to be part of his snare.

Her attention moved over them all, and her heart jumped in her chest at the sight of one person in particular. Waiting for her, watching her, loving her.

Bellamy.

"We shall," she answered Lord Chilsten, blinking through her tears, unable to comprehend how Bellamy had organized such a momentous day without her knowing. Bringing everyone she loved to Grafton so he could marry her.

She walked up the aisle, and the sight of little

Alice, soon to be her stepdaughter, made her tears fall quicker. She reached out to the little girl, taking her hand as she passed and bringing her with her to stand beside Bellamy.

Lord Chilsten gave her hand to Lord Lupton-Gage, and she shook her head, unable to comprehend, to understand. "Bellamy," she marveled, reaching up to clasp his face. "What are you doing?" she asked him, laughing.

He pulled her into his arms, holding her tight. "I'm going to marry you, Miss Hall. Now, before anything else can keep us apart."

She looked back at all their friends, many of whom were as teary as she was. "But you're in mourning. I just read the news today. I'm so sorry."

He shook his head, halting her words. "I will not mourn a woman who would have danced a jig upon my grave if she could. I will continue my life, marry the love of my life and never look back. That is what I want if that is what you want too?" he asked her.

So much happiness thrummed through her she thought she would burst. Reign reached for him, kissing him, having missed him so very much it hurt.

"It is what I want. More than anything," she answered, her heart full with wonder and hope for their future. A future with the man she loved above all else in the world. A man worth waiting for.

He nodded and turned to the reverend. "Please proceed," he ordered, a commanding lord to his very core.

The reverend cleared his throat and proclaimed to all, "We are gathered here today ..."

Dear Reader,

Thank you for taking the time to read *Brazen Rogue*! I hope you enjoyed the eighth book in my Wayward Woodvilles series!

I'm forever grateful to my readers, and if you're able, I would appreciate an honest review of *Brazen Rogue*. As they say, feed an author, leave a review!

Alternatively, you can keep in contact with me by visiting my website, subscribing to my newsletter or following me online. You can contact me at www.tamaragill.com.

Tamara Gill

Don't Miss Tamara's Other Romance Series

The Wayward Yorks

A Wager with a Duke

My Reformed Rogue

Wild, Wild, Duke

The Wayward Woodvilles

A Duke of a Time

On a Wild Duke Chase

Speak of the Duke

Every Duke has a Silver Lining

One Day my Duke Will Come

Surrender to the Duke

My Reckless Earl

Brazen Rogue

The Notorious Lord Sin

Wicked in My Bed

Royal House of Atharia

To Dream of You

A Royal Proposition

Forever My Princess

Only an Earl Will Do

Only a Duke Will Do

Only a Viscount Will Do

Only a Marquess Will Do

Only a Lady Will Do

A Time Traveler's Highland Love

To Conquer a Scot

To Save a Savage Scot

To Win a Highland Scot

A Stolen Season

A Stolen Season

A Stolen Season: Bath

A Stolen Season: London

Scandalous London

A Gentleman's Promise

A Captain's Order

A Marriage Made in Mayfair

High Seas & High Stakes

His Lady Smuggler

Her Gentleman Pirate

A Wallflower's Christmas Wreath

Daughters Of The Gods

Banished

Guardian

Fallen

Stand Alone Books

Defiant Surrender

A Brazen Agreement

To Sin with Scandal

Outlaws

About the Author

Tamara is an Australian author who grew up in an old mining town in country South Australia, where her love of history was founded. So much so, she made her darling husband travel to the UK for their honeymoon, where she dragged him from one historical monument and castle to another.

A mother of three, her two little gentlemen in the making, a future lady (she hopes) keep her busy in the real world, but whenever she gets a moment's peace she loves to write romance novels in an array of genres, including regency, medieval and time travel.

www.ingramcontent.com/pod-product-compliance
Lightning Source LLC
Chambersburg PA
CBHW070559120726
47909CB00007B/2390

* 9 7 8 0 6 4 5 7 2 5 7 8 0 *